PENGUIN BOOKS

THE STONE GODS

'Playful but impassioned . . . funny and beautiful' *The Times*

'In *The Stone Gods* she has surpassed herself. Soaringly imaginative and heartbreakingly beautiful . . . Winterson's writing is transcendent' *Metro*

'Crackling dialogue moves things right along, the surface of her tale scintillates. Underneath it, things are deadly serious'
Ursula K. Le Guin, *Guardian*

'This strange and beautiful love story . . . The fantastical tale is set in a distant, skillfully imagined future world and provides a brightly funny, creative and thoughtful read that will keep you engrossed' *New Woman*

'Witty, full of maverick spirit and ultimately encouraging' *Herald*

'This witty, challenging and thought-provoking novel should be essential reading for anyone concerned with how we live and how we might survive' *Daily Mail*

'Often very funny . . . Her imagination soars and, while the voyage is vertiginous, it is a journey worth taking' *Sunday Business Post*

'A sharply witty, emotional fable' *Harper's Bazaar*

'A humorous, mischievous and often perverse work laden with energy, adventure and rebellion – and, in particular, hope'
Sunday Independent

'Playful, passionate and often very funny' *Bella*

'This is a writer who always has something to say, something important, and ultimately that is what has always given her work the kind of passion so few writers today possess' *Scotsman*

ABOUT THE AUTHOR

Jeanette Winterson OBE, whose writing has won the Whitbread Award for Best First Novel, the John Llewellyn Rhys Memorial Prize and the E.M. Forster Award, is the author of some of the most purely imaginative and pleasurable novels of recent times, from *Oranges Are Not The Only Fruit* to her first book for children, *Tanglewreck*. She is also the author of the essays *Art Objects*.

Visit her website at www.jeanettewinterson.com

Read more at www.myspace.com/thestonegodsbook

The Stone Gods

JEANETTE WINTERSON

PENGUIN BOOKS

PENGUIN BOOKS

Published by the Penguin Group
Penguin Books Ltd, 80 Strand, London WC2R 0RL, England
Penguin Group (USA) Inc., 375 Hudson Street, New York, New York 10014, USA
Penguin Group (Canada), 90 Eglinton Avenue East, Suite 700, Toronto, Ontario, Canada M4P 2Y3
(a division of Pearson Penguin Canada Inc.)
Penguin Ireland, 25 St Stephen's Green, Dublin 2, Ireland
(a division of Penguin Books Ltd)
Penguin Group (Australia), 250 Camberwell Road, Camberwell, Victoria 3124, Australia
(a division of Pearson Australia Group Pty Ltd)
Penguin Books India Pvt Ltd, 11 Community Centre, Panchsheel Park, New Delhi – 110 017, India
Penguin Group (NZ), 67 Apollo Drive, Rosedale, North Shore 0632, New Zealand
(a division of Pearson New Zealand Ltd)
Penguin Books (South Africa) (Pty) Ltd, 24 Sturdee Avenue, Rosebank, Johannesburg 2196,
South Africa

Penguin Books Ltd, Registered Offices: 80 Strand, London WC2R 0RL, England

www.penguin.com

First published by Hamish Hamilton 2007
Published in Penguin Books 2008

1

Copyright © Jeanette Winterson, 2007

The moral right of the author has been asserted

Set in 11/13 pt PostScript Monotype Bembo
Typeset by Rowland Phototypesetting Ltd, Bury St Edmunds, Suffolk
Printed in Great Britain by Clays Ltd, St Ives plc

All rights reserved
Without limiting the rights under copyright reserved above, no part of this publication may be
reproduced, stored in or introduced into a retrieval system, or transmitted, in any form or by
any means (electronic, mechanical, photocopying, recording or otherwise), without the prior
written permission of both the copyright owner and the above publisher of this book.

ISBN-13: 978-0-14-103696-0

www.greenpenguin.co.uk

Penguin Books is committed to a sustainable future
for our business, our readers and our planet.
The book in your hands is made from paper
certified by the Forest Stewardship Council.

This book is to my oldest friends – Philippa Brewster, Vicky Licorish, Henri Llewelyn Davies, Mona Howard, Peggy Reynolds, Beeban Kidron, Phillippa Giles, and Ruth Rendell. And to Ali Smith, who came later, and to Deborah Warner, always.

Planet Blue

This new world weighs a yatto-gram.

But everything is trial-size; tread-on-me tiny or blurred-out-of-focus huge. There are leaves that have grown as big as cities, and there are birds that nest in cockleshells. On the white sand there are long-toed clawprints deep as nightmares, and there are rock pools in hand-hollows finned by invisible fish.

Trees like skyscrapers, and housing as many. Grass the height of hedges, nuts the swell of pumpkins. Sardines that would take two men to land them. Eggs, pale-blue-shelled, each the weight of a breaking universe.

And, underneath, mushrooms soft and small as a mouse ear. A crack like a cut, and inside a million million microbes wondering what to do next. Spores that wait for the wind and never look back.

Moss that is concentrating on being green.

A man pushes forward with a microphone – 'And is there oxygen?' Yes, there is. 'And fresh water?' Abundant. 'And no pollution?' None. Are there minerals? Is there gold? What's the weather like? Does it rain a lot? Has anyone tried the fish? Are there any humans? No, there are not any humans. Any intelligent life at all?

Depends what you mean by intelligent. There is something there, yes, and it's very big and very good at its job.

A picture of a scaly-coated monster with metal-plated

jaws appears on the overhead screen. The crowd shrieks and swoons. No! Yes! No! Yes!

The most efficient killing machine ever invented before gunpowder. Not bad for a thing with a body the size of a stadium and a brain the size of a jam-jar.

I am here today to answer questions: 'The lady in pink –'

'Are these monsters we can see vegetarian?'

'Ma'am, would you be vegetarian with teeth like that?'

It's the wrong answer. I am here to reassure. A scientist steps forward. That's better. Scientists are automatically reassuring.

This is a very exciting, and very reassuring, day.

We are here today to witness the chance of a lifetime. The chance of many lifetimes. The best chance we have had since life began. We are running out of planet and we have found a new one. Through all the bright-formed rocks that jewel the sky, we searched until we found the one we will call home. We're moving on, that's all. Everyone has to do that some time or other, sooner or later, it's only natural.

My name is Billie Crusoe.

'Excuse me, is your name Billie Crusoe?'

'That's me.'

'From Enhancement Services?'

'Yes, Every Day a New Day.' (As we say in Enhancement.)

'Can you tell viewers how the new planet will affect their lives?'

'Yes, I can. The new planet offers us the opportunity to do things differently. We've had a lot of brilliant successes here on Orbus — well, we are the success story of the universe, aren't we? I mean to say, no other planet hosts human life.'

The interviewer nods and smiles vigorously.

'But we have taken a few wrong turnings. Made a few mistakes. We have limited natural resources at our disposal, and a rising population that is by no means in agreement as to how our world as a whole should share out these remaining resources. Conflict is likely. A new planet means that we can begin to redistribute ourselves. It will mean a better quality of life for everyone — the ones who leave, and the ones who stay.'

'So a win-win situation?'

'That's right, winning numbers all the way.'

Through the golden arches that are the city gates, the President of the Central Power is arriving. The arches stand like angels, their wings folded back against the lesser lights of the skyline.

The laser-gates, which look so solid, appear and disappear, like the wall that rings the city, a visible and invisible sign of progress and power.

Look in the light — the slight shimmer is their long energy. They are the aura of the city: emblem and warning, its halo and shield.

The President's cavalcade has reached the Circle. Flags, carpets, flowers, flunkeys, hitmen, pressmen, frontmen, back-up, support, medics, techies, crew, rig, lights, sound, real-time, archive, relay, vox-pop, popcorn, polish, makeup, dust-down, ready, green — GO.

The President is making a speech. The Central Power has funded the space mission for hundreds of years, and it is understood that any discoveries belong to us. He compares us to the men who found the Indies, the Americas, the Arctic Circle; he becomes emotional, he reaches for a line of poetry. For a moment, there it is, in handwriting that nobody can read, slanting under the images of Planet Blue – *She is all States, all Princes I* . . .

The President is making a speech.

Unique moment for mankind . . . unrivalled opportunity . . . war averted . . . summit planned between the Central Power, Eastern Caliphate, and our friends in the Sino-Mosco Pact. Peaceful compromise promised. New planets for old. Full pictures and information across the twenty-two geo-cities of the Central Power by tomorrow morning. New colonizing mission being made ready. Monsters will be humanely destroyed, with the possible exception of scientific capture of one or two types for the Zooeum.

Into the Circle come the spacemen themselves, in shiny titanium pressure suits, oversize helmets under their arms. These are men glamorous as comets, trailing fame in fire-tails.

There's a robot with them – well, a Robo *sapiens*, incredibly sexy, with that look of regret they all have before they are dismantled. It's policy; all information-sensitive robots are dismantled after mission, so that their data cannot be accessed by hostile forces. She's been across the universe, and now she's going to the recycling unit. The great thing about robots, even these Robo *sapiens*, is that nobody feels sorry for them. They are only machines.

She stands there, while the silver-suited saviours shake the President's hand. She's going to tell us all about the chemical and mineral composition of the new planet, its atmospheric readings, its possible history and potential evolution. Then, when the public part is done, she'll go backstage, transfer all her data, and open her power cells until her last robot flicker.

The End.

It's a kind of suicide, a kind of bleeding to death, but they show no emotion because emotions are not part of their programming.

Amazing to look so convincing and be nothing but silicon and a circuit-board.

She glances over to the Support Stand and catches my eye. I can't help blushing. I think she has read my mind. They can do that.

This is a great day for science. The last hundred years have been hell. The doomsters and the environmentalists kept telling us we were as good as dead and, hey presto, not only do we find a new planet, but it is perfect for new life. This time, we'll be more careful. This time we will learn from our mistakes. The new planet will be home to the universe's first advanced civilization. It will be a democracy – because whatever we say in public, the Eastern Caliphate isn't going to be allowed within a yatto-mile of the place. We'll shoot 'em down before they land. No, we won't shoot them down, because the President of the Central Power has just announced a new world programme of No War. We will not shoot down the Eastern Caliphate, we will robustly repel them.

The way the thinking is going in private, we'll leave this run-down rotting planet to the Caliphate and the SinoMosco Pact, and they can bomb each other to paste while the peace-loving folks of the Central Power ship civilization to the new world.

★

The new world – El Dorado, Atlantis, the Gold Coast, Newfoundland, Plymouth Rock, Rapanaui, Utopia, Planet Blue. Chanc'd upon, spied through a glass darkly, drunken stories strapped to a barrel of rum, shipwreck, a Bible Compass, a giant fish led us there, a storm whirled us to this isle. In the wilderness of space, we found . . .

My name is Billie Crusoe. Here comes my boss, Manfred. He's the kind of man who was born to rise and rise: a human elevator.

'Billie, have you voiced through the downloads?'

'Yes, everything is there – sketches, diagrams, and a step-by-step explanation of how Planet Blue will change all our lives.'

'We have to present this positively.'

'It is positive, isn't it? Are you saying there are presentation problems with the chance that everyone is dying for?'

'Don't use the word "dying".'

'But Orbus is dying.'

'Orbus is not dying. Orbus is evolving in a way that is hostile to human life.'

'OK, so it's the planet's fault. We didn't do anything, did we? Just fucked it to death and kicked it when it wouldn't get up.'

'I know how you feel. I don't say you're entirely wrong in your analysis, but that isn't the way we can present the situation. The President has sent a memo this morning to instruct Enhancement Services and Media Services to work together on this. We don't want any stupid questions – any difficulties. The last thing the Central Power needs now is any unrest of our own. There will be trouble enough with the Caliphate and the Pact.'

'Because you're not giving a ride to either the Believers or the Collective?'

'When did they ever do anything for us?'

The Central Power is trying to live responsibly on a crowded planet, and that bunch are still scanning the skies for God, and draining the last drops of oil out of the ground. They can go to Hell.'

Manfred looked down at my notebook. He frowned his older-man-thinker-type-sexy frown. 'Billie, if you weren't so eccentric, you'd fit in better here. Why are you writing in a notebook? Nobody reads and writes any more – there's no need. Why can't you use a SpeechPad like everybody else?'

'Notebook. Pencil. They have an old-fashioned charm that I like.'

'And I like the present just as it is. You still living in that bio-bubble thing?'

'You mean the farm? Of course I am. If I'd been able to make it pay I wouldn't be working for you. But a world that clones its meat in the lab and engineers its crops underground thinks natural food is dirty and diseased.'

'It is.'

'Yeah. And pigs are planes. So the farm is leased to Living Museum and I am enslaved to you.'

'You don't get many scientists coming across to work in Enhancement . . . It's not exactly a career move.'

I had a feeling that something else was here – one of those ice-bound conversations that skate over the corpse in the lake. 'Is there a problem with my work?'

Manfred shrugged. 'Like I said, a Science Service high-flyer doesn't need to take a job with Enhancement.'

'You work for Enhancement.'

He was getting impatient. 'Billie, I'm going to be running the whole shooting match within two years. I have a graph. I have a Promotion Plan. I'm heading for the top floor.' (Yep, there he goes, Penthouse Man.) 'You aren't heading anywhere. You could have been promoted to Management within six months, but you're still on the ground, visiting people in their homes.'

'That's me, a cross between a District Nurse and an Insurance Salesman.'

'What's a District Nurse?'

'Never mind. History is a hobby of mine. It's not illegal, and neither is the farm, and neither is wanting a simple life. No graph, no Promotion Plan. OK?'

'OK. OK.'

He held up his hands. He turned to leave. 'Oh, you should move your Solo. Enforcement just gave you a ticket.'

'But I have a permit!'

'Take it up with Enforcement.'

'Manfred, this has been going on for a year – I clear them, they start again. I'm not paranoid, but if someone is out to get me, I would like to know.'

'No one is out to get you. But move the Solo. I would if I were you.'

He swung his handsome body and handsome head out and away to higher things.

Manfred is one of those confident men who have had themselves genetically Fixed as late-forties. Most men prefer to Fix younger than that, and there are no women who Fix past thirty. 'The DNA Dynasty', they called us, when the first generation of humans had successful recoding. Age is information failure. The body loses fluency. Command stations no longer connect with satellite stations. Relay breaks down. The body is designed to repair and renew itself, and most cells are only about a third as old as our birth years, but mitochondrial DNA is as old as we are, and has always accumulated mutations and distortions faster than DNA in the nucleus. For centuries we couldn't fix that – and now we can.

Science can't fix everything, though – women feel they have to look youthful, men less so, and the lifestyle programmes are full of the appeal of the older man. Everybody wants one – young girls and gay toyboys adore Manfred. His boyfriend has designed a robot that looks like him. Myself, I wouldn't be able to tell the difference.

I went downstairs, through the clotted ranks of Security and Support, officially known as Enforcement Services and Enhancement Services, but the SS has a better ring to it than the EE. We work together a lot of the time, soft-cop hard-cop kind of thing. It's my job – that is, our job – in Enhancement to explain to people that they really do want to live their lives in a way that is good for them and good for the Community. Enforcement steps in when it doesn't quite work out.

I know all the guys in Enforcement. I wave and smile. They nod, and let me pass.

Outside, there's a line of Solos and a line of Limos.

S is for Solo – a single-seater solar-powered transport vehicle. L is for Limo, a multi-seater hydrogen hybrid. S is for short-distance. L is for long-distance. Single-letter recognition is taught in schools.

In front of one of these vehicles, and one only, a CanCop is punching numbers into the Coder wired into his arm. CanCops are always around for back-up at high-security events – all they are is robots, soup cans with the power of Arrest.

On one of the long line of vehicles – and only one, mine – a bright yellow laser-light is covering the windshield. That's my penalty notice. Unless I press the yellow button on the parking meter next to it, I will not be able to drive away because I will not be able to see out of my glass. It's a clever system – you have to accept guilt before you can drive away and protest your innocence.

P is for Parking Meter. Slide up to the kerb, get out, look around, and the shiny solar-powered parking meter says to you, in its shiny solar-powered parking-meter voice – *Hi there! You can park here for thirty minutes. I will bill your account directly. Welcome to the neighbourhood.*

The meter then photographs your licence plate, connects to your Parking Account, which you must keep in credit at all times, and sends a digital receipt to your HomeScreen or your WorkScreen, whichever you have nominated. That's all there is to it, unless you run late, in which case the meter will laser-light your windshield in such a way as to make it impossible for you to drive off without accepting the Penalty.

So here I am – and I've been booked, even though I have a great big permit on the front of the car, with the date and time of my arrival and the impressive symbol of the Central Power.

I have been booked – again. If I were the paranoid type, which I am, I might almost start to believe that . . . Believe what?

I wave my arms at the CanCop, and point to the permit. He shrugs his tin shoulders. The guys from Enforcement are laughing – it's true this kind of cock-up, or cop-up, happens all the time, and it's a bore but not a problem . . . The trouble is that, for me, it's becoming a big problem.

I get out my Omni – the phone that does everything – and it automatically accesses the Parking Bureau Help Line. A sympathetic face flashes up in blonde pixels on my phone. 'DUE TO . . .' I slam her off before she gets any further.

D is for Due to. Whenever anybody calls to complain, a sympathetic person – well, a sympathetic robot, actually, because they are programmed to be more sympathetic than persons. Anyway, this sympathetic robot says, 'DUE TO', and you know that due to a high volume of calls, due to heavy demand, due to staff shortages, due to difficulties, due to system failure, due to freak storms, due to little green men squatting the offices, well, DUE TO, nobody is going to speak to you, at least not in this lifetime.

Fuck it fuck it fuck it. F is for Fuck it.

And in the middle of this hi-tech, hi-stress, hi-mess life, F is for Farm. My farm. Twenty hectares of pastureland and arable, with a stream running through the middle like a memory. Step into that water and you remember everything, and what you don't remember, you invent.

My farm is the last of its line – like an ancient ancestor everyone forgot. It's a bio-dome world, secret and sealed: a message in a bottle from another time.

The soil is deep clay and the cattle make holes in it where they herd to feed. The holes fill with water, then ice over, and the birds crack open the ice to drink. The woodland belts that hold the fields are thick with branches thick with birds. At evening the sky above the wood is dark with the wings of birds.

The rough fences, the uneven ground, the tussocks of grass, the tiny blue violets that grow where the cattle go, the poppies that change the furrowed earth into a red sea that hares part. The distance the eye follows to whatever moves and dives, the life that fills every bit of uncultivated hedge and verge. The burrows, tunnels, nests, tree-hollows, wasp-balls, drilled-out holes of the water voles, otter sticks, toad stones, mice riddling the dry-stone walls, badger sets, molehills, fox dens, rabbit warrens, stoats brown in summer, ermine in winter, clean as bullets through the bank. The trout shy in the reeds. The carp dozing on the riverbed. Dragonflies like Annunciations. A kingfisher on wings of blue light. A green-headed duck and a white swan dropping under the white-foamed fall of the green water to the bottom of the clough where the frogs wait patiently to be in a fairytale.

There is no magic wand here. If I don't move the Solo in the next five minutes, yellow will change to orange will change to red, not the way the sun changes, to mark the day, but so that my fine gets bigger. Press the button, Billie. Press the bloody button. B is for Billie, button and bloody.

THANK YOU! says the parking meter. *You are ready to drive away.*

There won't be any parking meters on the new blue planet. That alone makes the visit worth the trip.

I have an appointment today with a woman who wants to be genetically reversed to twelve years old to stop her husband running after schoolgirls. It's possible, but it's illegal. She wants to take her case to the Court of Human Rights. She's already seen a psychiatrist and a Consultant specializing in Genetics. Now she has to talk to me, woman to woman, because Enhancement is here to Listen when You have Problems.

I key in my destination co-ordinates, and the Solo makes its way across to the Business Lane. This is peak-hour driving and I am paying the price mile by mile. In the Leisure Lane, nobody is paying at all but, then, nobody is moving either.

The first pictures of Planet Blue are beginning to appear on the smart-skins of the buildings. It's as though we are driving straight towards it. There it is, pristine, diamond-cut, and the zooms show miles and miles of empty beauty. Everyone on the highway is watching. It doesn't matter: magnetic rebuff stops anyone driving into anyone else. We just stay in line and get there some day. Yeah, we'll get there some day, blue planet, silver stars.

The Solo is beeping. Voice Announce tells me to turn right, and the wall-screen on the corner of the road flashes a picture of a bell. This must be Belle Vue Drive. Etymology was one of the victims of State-approved mass illiteracy. Sorry, a move towards a more integrated, user-friendly day-to-day information and communications system. (Voice and pictures, yes; written words, no.)

As I make the turn, I drive straight towards a BeatBot.

BeatBots: direct descendants of a low-paid State Functionary that used to be called a Traffic Warden. As everyone knew, these types were inhuman, and it made more sense to build them than to hire them, so as soon as the technology became available, that was what we did.

The BeatBot waves me over, and buzzes out his question in his trademark synthesized voice that sounds like wasps in a dustbin. BeatBots don't have to sound like this, but they do: Why was I hesitating on a busy turn from a main highway?

I tell him I was just waiting to see the road sign. He mumbles something into the radio that is an extension of his chin, and the next thing I know, a couple of Nifties are checking out the underside of the car with mirrors.

Nifties: annoying little micro-Bots that scuttle around in drains and fix underfloor heating. Most people keep a couple in the car in case they want something picked up off the floor or need a foot massage. Nifties have no personality, and they look like a box on wheels with a retractable aerial at each corner. They were designed for busy people on the move – which is all of us, because staying still is so last-century.

'What's the problem?' I ask the Bot, but he won't answer, because BeatBots have very limited powers of speech.

I must not get paranoid – Bots are a typical happening on a typical road here in Tech City, because Tech City is where every single robot in the twenty-two geo-cities of the Central Power is designed and made. Naturally, or unnaturally, I suppose, we have a lot of them.

R is for Robot.

There's Kitchenhand for the chores, Flying Feet to run errands or play football with the kids. Garagehand – that's the big hairy one that's good with a spanner. There's Lend-a-Hand too, for the temporarily unpartnered.

We have Robo-paws, the perfect pet – depending on your definition of perfect. We have TourBots, for hire when you visit a new place and need someone to show you round. We have bottom of the range LoBots, who have no feet because they spend all their time on their knees cleaning up. And we have BeatBots. Yeah.

Mine has finished chewing over the car, and issued an Offence Code. I don't know what my offence is – but I do know it's impossible to argue with a BeatBot. I'll have to take it up with the Computer later.

The BeatBot shuffles off in his oversize nano-parka with intelligent hood. The hood is the bit that processes information – the rest of the Bot is just a moving lump of metal – which is what all robots are, when you come down to it, until the big breakthrough.

Robo *sapiens*.

As far away from a BeatBot as Neanderthal Man is from us. No, I have to revise that because we are regressing. Oh, yes, it's true – we have no need for brains so our brains are shrinking. Not all brains, just most people's brains – it's an inevitable part of progress.

Meanwhile, the Robo *sapiens* is evolving.

The first artificial creature that looks and acts human, and that can evolve like a human – within limits, of course.

There are not very many of them, and they are fabulously expensive to make. If you want the ultimate piece of personal-wealth display, you get a Robo *sapiens*. The President of the Central Power keeps a pair who work as his PA and BodyGuard. They remember everything – faces, information, numbers, conversation – and they can make connections. These are robots who join the dots. Ask them for advice, and they will give it to you: impartial advice based on everything that can be known about the situation.

Ask them what you were doing this time two years ago, and they will tell you. Ask them what you ate at your wife's first G party and they have the menu off by heart. Except that they don't have hearts.

★

Heartless. Gorgeous. Even so, I have never seen one as impressive as the one they took with them to Planet Blue. She was built especially for the job, but did she need to be so beautiful too?

Inter-species sex is punishable by death.

Looking down the street at the numbers, it seems that my client is throwing a G party. In the past, people had birthdays. I have charted all of that through the Central Archive. Now birthdays don't matter because they mark the passing of the years, and for us years don't pass in the way that they once did. G is the day and year you genetically fix. It's a great day to celebrate.

I park the Solo on the meter outside the house. *Hi there!* says the hateful familiar voice. I ignore it and key in my override code, which Enhancement officers can do when on work-related calls. *All set! See you later!*

I kick it for fun. Nothing happens, of course.

The house – number twenty-nine – is festooned with pink pumped-up balloons. There are enough balloons on this house to qualify it for personal take-off. Batting aside the ones in my way, like giant mammaries, I lift the knocker.

A pink LoBot opens the door and brushes my (black) trainers with a pink brush.

Ducking under more pink balloons to follow the LoBot, I am able to enter the rosy sitting room. It should be a sitting room, in that it is off the hall and on the ground floor, but it is faked out like a teenager's bedroom, and stuffed with celebrity holograms the way people in the past used to stuff their lounges with china ornaments. The problem with the hologram craze is that even if you scale them down you're still surrounded by dwarf-size replicas of movie stars and pop idols. Of course, you can walk right through them, but I find it creepy. This place is like a Hall of Fame. I can hardly shift for three-foot-tall Goliaths of the film industry. The LoBot is at just the right height to dust them top to bottom. She gets out a pink duster and sets to work.

'I love celebrity,' says my client, Mrs Mary McMurphy, 'but they need dusting. Even holograms attract dust. A lot of people don't realize that so they get allergies – from the dust, y'know, trapped in the hologram.'

Celebrities are under pressure, no doubt about it. We are all young and beautiful now, so how can they stay ahead of the game? Most of them have macro-surgery. Their boobs swell like beach balls, and their dicks go up and down like beach umbrellas. They are surgically stretched to be taller, and steroids give them muscle-growth that turns them into star-gods. Their body parts are bio-enhanced, and their hair can do clever things like change colour to match their outfits. They are everything that science and money can buy.

'I want to look like her,' says Mrs McMurphy.

'Like who?'

'Like Little Señorita.'

Little Señorita is a twelve-year-old pop star who has Fixed herself rather than lose her fame. She sees no point in growing up when she is famous for not being grown-up. Understandably, as she has no talent, she wants to live in the moment for as long as she can.

Her parents support her. Her boyfriend says he's delighted.

'My husband is mad about Little Señorita. I want to be her.'

'Are you sure you want to be her for the rest of your life?'

'I can change later if it doesn't work out.'

Yes and no. Genetic reversal has strange effects on the body. The last time it was done, the reversal couldn't be contained, and the girl got younger and younger until she was a six-feet-tall six-month-old baby.

Fixing is simple. Unfixing to age naturally is pretty simple, though it is only ever done for medical research. I am explaining this to Mrs McMurphy and getting nowhere.

'My husband likes girls.'

'Legal sex starts at fourteen,' I reply.

'But everybody does it younger. Y'know that!'

'Does he have underage sex at home?'

'Oh, no, he always goes out. But I don't want to lose him.'

'Why not?'

She seems baffled by this question, and shifts among her cushions the colour of Turkish Delight, then hitches her school uniform, her pink school uniform, slightly higher. Any higher and it will just be a scarf round her neck, or maybe a hairband.

'Do you think you can stop him having sex with young girls by becoming one yourself?'

'Y'know, that's not my aim. He can do what he likes as long as he doesn't do it in the house,' she makes him sound like a golden retriever, 'and as long as he comes home now and again and does it with me.' He is a golden retriever. 'We don't have sex any more. He says I'm too old.'

A pair of Kitchenhands, got up to look like pink rubber gloves, comes into the sitting room, bearing two tall tumblers of a foaming liquid.

'I swear by Nitrogen Ginseng,' says my client.

While Mrs McMurphy takes and drinks hers eagerly, I take the opportunity to look more closely.

I guess she has been Fixed at twenty-four. Now that everyone is young and beautiful, a lot of men are chasing girls who are just kids. They want something different when everything has become the same.

'I need to speak to your husband too.'

'He's not here.'

'Well, he should be here. This is an official appointment. Where is he?'

'He's at the Peccadillo.'

She has the grace to blush – no, I think she's blushing because it matches her outfit and the cushions and the wallpaper. It's all one childish, knowing, pre-teen turn-on. There is no point in staying. I gather my things and get up to leave. The hovering Kitchenhands lace their separate fingers and park quietly on top of a pot plant. The LoBot scurries towards the door.

'Are you excited about Planet Blue?' I ask Mrs McMurphy, by way of ending the conversation.

She looks vague and smiles. 'Yeah, y'know, it's a great idea. I'm entering the celebrity competition to win a trip. The beaches look amazing.'

Outside, the windshield of my Solo is flashing yellow. What? This is crazy. Have all the stupid parking meters gone crazy? I don't even bother to ring the blonde pixellated robot on the DUE TO line. I ring Manfred. He sounds shifty.

'Have you got all you need for your report?'

'I have to find the husband. He's at the Peccadillo.'

'You can't go there in work time.'

'Then I can't make my report. I need to speak to her husband.'

'We have to nail this, Billie. Media want to interview her, and they'll need your notes before the story breaks. This Human Rights case is going to be the Next Big Thing after Planet Blue.'

'You mean that when we're bored to death with the news of a new world, the one we dreamed about for millennia, we'll go back to sex stories?'

'You're always so negative!'

'Sorry, you're right, it's going to be wonderful here on Planet Lolita. Why go anywhere else?'

'It's not your job to moralize.'

'So I'm going to the Peccadillo?'

'Yes.'

'And you'll clear my parking?'

'Yes.'

We both hang up trying to hang up first. It's time I found a new job. Even polishing LoBots would be better than this. Even getting a job as a BeatBot would be better than this.

At the Peccadillo parking is private, so I drive underground, leave the keys with Security, and take the elevator up to the Members' Floor. A hunchback bows me in.

There are a couple of translucents serving behind the bar.

Translucents are see-through people. When you fuck them you can watch yourself doing it. It's pornography for introverts.

Peccadillo is a perverts' bar, and we're all perverts now. By that I mean that making everyone young and beautiful also made us all bored to death with sex. All men are hung like whales. All women are tight as clams below and inflated like lifebuoys above. Jaws are square, skin is tanned, muscles are toned, and no one gets turned on. It's a global crisis. At least, it's a crisis among the cities of the Central Power. The Eastern Caliphate has banned Genetic Fixing, and the SinoMosco Pact does not make it available to all its citizens, only to members of the ruling party and their favourites. That way the leaders look like star-gods and the rest look like shit-shovellers. They never claimed to be a democracy.

The Central Power is a democracy. We look alike, except for rich people and celebrities, who look better. That's what you'd expect in a democracy.

So, sexy sex is now about freaks and children. If you want to work in the sex industry, you get yourself cosmetically altered in shape and size. Giantesses are back in business. Grotesques earn good money. Kids under ten are known as veal in the trade.

Today at the Peccadillo it's a Veal Special so I'm not surprised to see a blond-haired guy, who looks like a golden retriever, heading for the Jacuzzi with a ten-year-old boy on his shoulders and a ten-year-old girl in his arms. Both of them are Caliphate kids. We buy them. We wouldn't do it to kids born in the Central Power because (a) it's illegal and (b) we're civilized.

As I hurry across the floor, my way is barred by an enormous woman with one leg, hopping along on a diamond-studded crutch. I am on a level with her impressive breasts – more so, because where I would normally expect to find a nipple, I find a mouth. Her breasts are smiling, and so is she.

'Are you hungry for a playmate?'

'No, thank you. I'm just visiting the Jacuzzi.'

'Oh, don't waste your time in there. That's for kids. Come to the Fun Room. I can take four men at a time – front, rear, here and here.' She pats her accommodating breast-mouths, or is it mouth-breasts?

'I'm a girl.'

'Yeah, but you can watch, and when the boys are done, we can have some FUN. You're not straight, are you?'

'Not exactly.'

'Well, then, come along.'

'Look, I have to catch up with a guy who looks like a golden retriever.'

'Does he work here? I don't recall a Dog Man. We have a Dog Woman, hounds included.'

'No. He just looks like a golden retriever.'

'Cute. Well, when he's done what a dog has to do, you know where to find me. Just listen for the tap, tap, tap.'

She puts her crutch down and swings off. The one leg is for easier access.

Am I a prude? Am I a moralist? Am I letting life's riches pass me by? Why do I want to go for a walk in the woods and say nothing until you turn to me and I take your face in both hands and kiss you?

I don't even know who you are.

A voice comes from behind me. 'Who R U? Whaddya want?'

Big questions. For a moment I don't know what to say. Then I remember. 'I want to talk to Mr McMurphy.'

'You can't. He's busy.'

I explain my situation. The boss-guy, bouncer-guy, whatever he is, nods and says he'll pass the message on.

'Well, go in there and ask him why he wants his wife to look like Little Señorita.'

'You stupid or what? We all want our wives to look like Little Señorita.'

'Why is that?'

'Coz she's hot, and this town is frigid.'

'Do you have a wife?'

'Not yet. I'm getting one from the Eastern Caliphate – it'll be legal, believe me, but she's nine years old and I'm gonna Fix her.'

'Children cannot be Fixed. That is the law.'

'Little Señorita –'

'Is fighting a legal battle, which she will lose.'

'You don't know that.'

'You don't know that she will win.'

'Oh, no? There's plenty of guys who want her to win, and you know what? They're all in the gang. Judges, politicians, you name it.'

But I don't want to name it.

'It's like every other Civil Rights and Equal Rights battle, OK? You had Blacks at one time. You had Semites at one time. You had mixed marriages, you had gays. All legal. No problem. We're just victims of prejudice and out-of-date laws.'

'It's called "paedophilia".'

'That's just a word, like "homosexual".'

'No, it's not a word like "homosexual", it's a word like "goatfucker".'

'What's a goat?'

Let me try again. 'The kids are too young.'

'Sure not. They love it. Listen . . .'

He props open the door into the Jacuzzi room with his jackboot.

I can hear kids splashing and playing. I push past him and look inside. Sure enough, the place is wet with kids running and diving and throwing themselves through the fountains and down the slides, and there are four guys with hard-ons like concrete breakers waiting to catch them.

'Mr McMurphy!' I shout. He turns and smiles his playboy smile. He comes over to the edge of the wet room, stroking himself. 'About your wife . . .'

'Yeah, whatever she wants, I'm behind her all the way. Her choice. I believe that women should make their own choices. Whatever she wants, all the way.'

The boss-guy, bouncer-guy manoeuvres me firmly out of the door and gives my bum a little squeeze. 'This is the future, honey.'

'Do you ever think about a world where there are no grown women at all? Just little girls?'

'Don't get me going. I'm on duty.'

I make my way back past the translucents, one of whom is doing his party trick with a Campari-soda. You can see the red going all the way down. So this is the future: girls Fixed at eight years old, maybe ten, hopefully twelve. Or will they want women's minds in girls' bodies and go for genetic reversal?

The future of women is uncertain. We don't breed in the womb any more, and if we aren't wanted for sex . . . But there will always be men. Women haven't gone for little boys. Women have a different approach. Surrounded by hunks, they look for 'the ugly man inside'. Thugs and gangsters, rapists and wife-beaters are making a comeback. They may smile like beach-boys, but they are pure shark.

So this is the future. F is for Future.

Out of the window, where it's going dark, I can see the laser-projection of Planet Blue. She needs us like a bed needs bedbugs. 'I'm sorry,' I say, to the planet that can't hear me. And I wish she could sail through space, unfurling her white clouds to solar winds, and find a new orbit, empty of direction, where we cannot go, and where we will never find her, and where the sea, clean as a beginning, will wash away any trace of humankind.

The phone rings – it's Manfred. He sounds excited. 'Pick up a new dress on your way home. Media wants a live TV interview with that Robo *sapiens* they're dismantling. You're going to front it. I want you to look good.'

'I already look good – we all look good.'

'Cut the crap, Billie – get the dress.'

He hangs up again.

This is worse than a bad relationship. Still, it's my job, while I have it, so without more ado I leave the Peccadillo and walk a few blocks to a chic clothes store. I should be glad to be shopping in work time, but I'm not glad about anything. In fact, I'm depressed, which is pretty much illegal. By that I mean that at the first sign of depression I, you, anyone is supposed to see their doctor and be referred to someone from Enhancement, but I am someone from Enhancement, and I am depressed.

I tried smiling, straightening my back and walking positively into the scented, mauve-coloured, cool interior of the fishpond-fitted intelligent shopping experience.

As soon as my dusty unacceptable feet triggered the sensor, Tasha's face appeared smiling on the wall. Tasha is in all the best women's clothing stores. It's a way of giving clone-clothing the exclusive but personal feel. 'Hi, Tasha,' I say, 'A112.'

'Hi, Billie, nice to see you. You look a little dusty.'

'I feel dusty. Can you find me something to wear? A dress?'

My number has already given Tasha my name, details, size, previous items bought – in fact, my entire shopping history since nappies.

'Let's see,' said Tasha, 'I'll go into Wardrobe, and flash a few things on the wall, and if you like any, we'll send them right up to try.'

In a few seconds a selection of summer dresses and strappy sandals replaces Tasha's face on the wall.

'I think you'd look good in numbers one, three and six with matching footwear,' she says from somewhere, nowhere.

She is right, of course, because computers are good at matching things – including people and their clothes. Mind you, as we all look more or less alike, and there are only two sizes, Model Thin and Model Thinner, it isn't hard.

'I'll send up one and six MT size,' says Tasha, before I have time to make a pretence of being part of this intelligent shopping experience. Never mind, the clothes are nice.

When I try on number six, it fits perfectly. I look wonderful in a normal sort of way because I always do look wonderful.

'You look wonderful,' says Tasha, purring like the computer cat that has just appeared next to her. 'Smartie thinks you look wonderful too.'

We all love Smartie, who is there to purr us on when we can't make up what is left of our minds. Some marketing guru realized long ago that animals, even fake ones, make people feel smug, good and relaxed. We feel like

Tasha and Smartie really care, and who am I to say that they don't?

'Your size used to be MTT,' says Tasha. 'Are you happy with the extra weight?'

'Yes, I like it,' I say.

'I like it too,' says Tasha, taking her cue and, really, what is the difference between a size eight and a size ten? Only this: we still have a dieting industry.

Tasha, Smartie and I agree to charge the dress to my account, and I make a voluntary donation to Charity of the Month, which this month is Apes in the Wild.

'There isn't any Wild,' I say.

'Exactly so,' says Tasha. 'The money is to create a strip of Wild, and then put Apes in it.'

I don't know where the money goes, but everyone likes to give to charity: it shows we care.

'Anything else I can do for you today?' asks Tasha.

'Lipstick?'

'On me. My pleasure. I'll drop it in the basket by the door. Goodbye, Billie. See ya soon!'

Tasha disappears, leaving Smartie to wash himself. As I reach the door, my dress drops wrapped and ready into the Exit basket, and there is my lipstick in a bag on top. Very thoughtful of Tasha. Like a friend, I suppose.

I walk back towards the car park to pick up my Solo.

Guess what? The windshield is yellow. There's a code number flashing on it in black, like a demented hornet. As there is no parking meter, I have to key this code into my phone to drive away. It's what happens when you're caught on CCTV doing an illegal. But this isn't an illegal. This is private parking.

I am beginning to feel justifiable paranoia. I look around

for the cameras, not that you can ever see them. I am being watched, but that isn't strange. That's life. We're all used to it. What is strange is that I feel I am being watched. Staked out. Observed. But there's no one there.

I stand for a moment in the bleak and empty underground parking lot. I am human. I am thirty. I am alone.

I key in the ACCEPT code, and begin my way back to the office.

On the radio, all the talk is of the new blue planet.

You dreamed all your life there was somewhere to land, a place to lie down and sleep, with the sound of water nearby. You set off to find it, buying old maps and listening to travellers' tales, because you believed that the treasure was really there.

Here I am, dreaming blue but seeing red. There's a red duststorm beginning, like spider-mite, like ants, like things that itch and bite. No one has any idea where the red dust is coming from but it clogs the air-filtering systems, and since it started about two years ago, we are obliged to carry oxygen masks. This one might blow over or it might not.

As I close the air-vents on the Solo and switch to the compressed air in the cabin, I hear something on the radio about the arrest of twenty-five Unknowns. What are they saying? 'Caught in the space compound, attempting to sabotage the next mission to Planet Blue. All of them identity-closed X-Cits.'

I is for Identity. In the long past, governments could destroy your papers and rescind your passport. Then they learned how to freeze your assets and steal your cash. Now that we have no cash, just credit accounts, those can be barred, but the tough measure is Identity Closure. Simply, you no longer exist. You become an X-Cit, an ex-citizen. There will be no record of you ever having existed. You can't travel, you can't buy anything, you can't register for anything, you can't plead your case. You can't use what was your name. When you get out of jail, if you ever get out of jail, you will be micro-tagged for life as an Unknown. You see them sometimes, cleaning the streets, their taggers flashing at fifteen-minute intervals, checked and recorded by the satellite system that watches us more closely than God ever did.

Twenty-five Unknowns. The official line is that the Resistance has been smashed. There is no Resistance to the Central Power. That's why it seems to me to be useful to be able to read – if only between the lines.

Ahead of me are the huge double laser-arches that take me back into Tech City. You can see the giant golden Ms for miles, glittering under the sky, adapting to the weather.

Sometimes, for security reasons, there are long queues through the high, cathedral-like vaulted welcome into the capital.

But today we are all speeding under the golden arms of the arches into our city, into our lives, into the world that is a stream of information, ceaselessly collected and projected.

She is all States, all Princes I, Nothing else is.

Manfred, shirt perfectly cut to his pecs, is waiting for me.

'Congratulations, Billie. This is your lucky break. An in-depth special for *The One Minute Show*.'

'In depth? One Minute? Do you sense any conflict here, Manfred?'

'Don't make this difficult, Billie. All you have to do is

interview the Robo *sapiens*, and write a Download for after broadcast.'

'That's Media work, not my work.'

'Billie, you are standing at a Career Moment. Stop complaining and take your opportunity.'

'Why me?'

'The Robo *sapiens* had the idea herself. She thought you were impressive at the presentation this morning. Call it her Last Request. This is a poignant personal moment for her. They are draining her data right now.'

Manfred sets off down the corridor. How come progress has done nothing for the corridor? They have always looked like this – dead carpet, faceless doors, blank pictures, water-cooler, chocolate machine, signs for the restrooms and the elevators.

The free corridor soon becomes a pass-code corridor. Biometric sensors note Manfred's very presence, and the doors swing open.

Guards lounge against the walls, shaking themselves upright as Manfred appears. We go into a bright white room. Sitting in the centre is the Robo *sapiens*, dark hair falling across her face. Her arm is bare and strapped with wires. She looks like she's giving blood. I suppose she is – the data she stores is her life's blood, and when it's gone, so is she.

'Sorry, I can't shake hands.' She looks across at me, smiling.

'Billie, meet Spike – a legend in her own lifetime. Spike, this is Billie Crusoe, as requested, for your final interview.'

Manfred turns to the three lab scientists and addresses them briefly. They nod, and file out of the room. Manfred is smiling. 'The cam-host is set to record. Short interview, and we'll edit it later. Billie – did you buy the dress? Put it on! Buzz me when you're done. I have to authorize your release myself.'

'Am I in jail already?'

'And keep it light, upbeat, OK?'

He swings through the swing doors. We are alone.

Spike doesn't say anything, but she looks at me, and I know she'll be reading my data-chip implant. Everything about me is stored just above my wrist.

'I can't read your data,' she says, reading my mind instead. 'That function is passive while I'm draining.'

'How long will the draining take?'

'A few hours, including questions, then I'm done.'

'You were built entirely for the space mission, right?'

She nods and smiles. She is absurdly beautiful. I start to slip off my jeans and I feel her gaze as I stand in my bra and pants. Why am I embarrassed about taking off my clothes in front of a robot? I pull the dress over my head like a schoolgirl, untie my hair, and sit down. She is smiling, just a little bit, as though she knows her effect.

To calm myself down and appear in control I reverse the problem. 'Spike, you're a robot, but why are you such a drop-dead gorgeous robot? I mean, is it necessary to be the most sophisticated machine ever built and to look like a movie star?'

She answers simply: 'They thought I would be good for the boys on the mission.'

I am pondering the implications of this. Like a wartime pin-up? Like a live anti-depressant? Like truth is beauty, beauty truth? 'How good? I mean, I'm assuming you're not talking sexual services here.'

'What else is there to do in space for three years?'

'But inter-species sex is illegal.'

'Not on another planet it isn't. Not in space it isn't.'

'But you were also the most advanced member of the crew.'

'I'm still a woman.'

Manfred's voice comes booming into the room. 'This is not public-broadcast material.'

I get up to fetch some water, and as I pass Spike, I say, so low that she can barely hear me, 'Can we switch him blank?'

As I return with the water, she whispers, not looking at me. 'Red panel, blue relay.'

I do it.

'We're still on cam-cast.'

'What you did Disables Record.'

'So you had sex with spacemen for three years?'

'Yes. I used up three silicon-lined vaginas.'

There is a roar from Somewhere, like a dinosaur in space. Obviously Record has not Disabled. 'Sorry, Manfred!' I yell. 'I know this is a prime-time family show.'

While my voice is placating Manfred, my feelings are confused. I want to be outraged on this woman's behalf, but she isn't a woman, she's a robot, and isn't it better that they used a robot instead of dispatching a couple of sex-slaves?

And yet. And yet Robo *sapiens* are not us, but they may become a nearer relative than the ape.

'Humans share ninety-seven per cent of their genetic material with apes,' said Spike, 'but they feel no kinship.'

'Do we feel kinship with robots?'

'In time you will, as the differences between us decrease.'

I decide to ignore the vast implications of this statement as unsuitable for an In-depth One Minute Special. Instead I press Record and turn, smiling, to Spike. 'I have a question that will interest many people,' I say, knowing that nearly everyone would be much more interested to hear about robot-sex in space. 'If your data can be transferred, as is happening now, then why must we dismantle you when you cost so much to build?'

'I am not authorized to answer that question,' she says, with perfect robot control. Then she leans forward and takes my hand and she says, 'It is because I can never forget.'

'What? I don't understand. We take the data . . .'

'And I can recall it.'

'But you can't — it's vast, it's stored computer data. When it's downloaded, the host, the carrier, whatever you are, sorry, can be wiped clean. Why aren't you a machine for re-use?'

'Because I am not a machine.'

When she smiles it's like light at the beginning of the day. 'Robo *sapiens* were programmed to evolve . . .'

'Within limits.'

'We have broken those limits.'

Manfred comes slamming in through the slam doors. 'Would you ladies *please* stop this touching psychodrama, and get on with the interview? We go live in one hour.' He sits down in a corner, crossing his elegant linen-pressed legs.

He's here to stay. I have probably lost my job.

I turn back to Spike. She looks me calmly and clearly in the eye, and into my head, as though she were speaking, which she isn't, she says, 'Will you help me to escape?'

I said, 'Did I just hear you?' She nods. Then I say, out loud, 'Yes.'

'Yes what?' says Manfred, irritably.

'Yes, we're restarting the interview.'

I turn back, fully focused on those green liquid-crystal eyes. 'So tell me about Planet Blue. Tell me everything.'

She says, '*This new world weighs a yatto-gram . . .*

'*When we approached it, polar-swirled, white-whirled, diamond-blue, routed by rivers, we found a world still forming. There was evidence that carbon had once been the dominant gas, and after that methane and, finally, oxygen, thanks to the intervention of cynobacteria. Oxygen creates a planet receptive to our forms of life.*

'*Like Orbus, Planet Blue is made up of land and sea areas, with high mountain ranges and what appear to be frozen regions. We have landed two roving probes on the planet and expect a steady supply of data over the coming months.*

'*As you will see from the photographs, the planet is abundantly forested. Insect life, marine life and mammals are evident. It is strikingly similar to our own planet, sixty-five million years ago, with the exception of the dinosaurs, of which we have no record on Orbus.*'

'Ask her when we can start relocating,' shouted Manfred. 'We want the human story.'

'The answer to that question,' said Spike, carefully, 'is that we can leave tomorrow. There is oxygen, water, food and every other resource.'

'And there are monsters,' I said.

'Don't call them that,' barked Manfred, two strands of his impeccable hair now loose over his violet eyes. 'Do you want to put people off?'

'Would you like to live on Planet Blue?' I asked Spike.

'I would like to be part of the next exploratory mission, yes.'

'How do you feel about being dismantled? It's a kind of death, isn't it?'

'I think of it as recycling, which is what Nature does all the time. The natural world is abundant and extravagant, but nothing is wasted. The only waste in the Cosmos comes from human beings.'

'We can cut it right there,' said Manfred.

The alarm was going off. It was a red-alert pollution warning. The building would now seal itself and the air-conditioning would pump in pure oxygen.

'I hate those selfish, greedy, bigoted bastards,' said Manfred, getting up and coming over. 'What right have they to do this to us?'

'I presume you mean the Caliphate and the Pact?'

'Who else is destabilizing the world?'

'Well, we've done a pretty good job of it for as long as anyone can remember,' I say, knowing this is the wrong answer.

'Have you never heard of global responsibility? We are all of us on the planet obliged to tend the planet.'

I don't bother to answer. We made ourselves rich polluting the rest of the world, and now the rest of the world is polluting us.

'Carbon dioxide is five hundred and fifty parts per million,' said Spike. 'It's too late.'

'It is never too late!' said Manfred. 'That's delusional, depressive and anti-science. We have the best weather-shield in the world. We have slowed global warming. We have stabilized emissions. We have drained rising sea levels, we have replanted forests, we have synthesized food, ending centuries of harmful farming practices,' he glares at me again, 'we have neutralized acid rain, we have permanent refrigeration around the ice-caps, we no longer use oil, gasoline or petroleum derivatives. What more do you want?'

'I don't want anything,' said Spike, calmly. 'I am a robot.'

'If those out-of-control lunatics in the rest of the world would just get the message –'

'That when we destabilized the planet it was in the name of progress and economic growth. Now that they're doing it, it's selfish and it's suicide.'

'You think you're so smart, don't you?' said Manfred. 'But I live in the real world. We did what we did, sure, and when all the scientific data was in place –'

'When it was too late.'

Manfred ignored me, the way you do a street preacher, '– then we took full responsibility, and worked to put it right. Meanwhile, those backward sky-god worshippers and those stupid little slant-eyed clones – those guys are crippling us.'

'Well, Manfred, you can always put your name down for Planet Blue.'

'It'll be decades before that's viable.'

'We could go now,' said Spike.

Manfred started waving his arms like a wind turbine. 'We need infrastructure, buildings, services. If I'm going to live on a different planet, I want to do it properly. I want shops and hospitals. I'm not a pioneer. I like city life, like everyone likes city life. The Central Power believes that the biggest obstacle to mass migration will be setting up the infrastructure in time. We can't go back to the Bog Ages.'

'There won't be enough time,' said Spike. 'Either you go or you don't.'

'I'm sorry, but that doesn't accord with my brief,' said

Manfred, in a voice that ended the matter. He strode over to the window and looked down, frowning. 'There's red dust covering the place again. What the hell is that stuff?'

Manfred wasn't interested in us any more, so I said to Spike, 'What do you mean, just go?'

'Orbus has a projected remaining lifespan of around fifty years. The planet will continue, of course, but it will no longer be hospitable to life as we know it. We can continue here for some time after that, cooling our cities, and using developing technology, but the future is not sustainable. Nor is there time to develop Planet Blue in the way that the Central Power desires. Human beings will have to begin again.'

'With what?'

'With a pristine planet and abundant natural resources. It might be possible to develop a hi-tech, low-impact society, making the best of our mistakes here, and beginning again differently.'

'So it really is a second chance.'

'I think so.'

'Do people want to begin again? They imagine business as usual but with a barbecue on the beach at the end of the day. They think plasma buildings and genetic Fixing, but with better scenery and no foreigners.'

As the ALL-CLEAR sounded, the lab technicians came back in, and Manfred motioned for me to leave.

'What time are you through here?' he asked the men, as they sat down at their screens.

'Maybe three or four hours, then we'll run her down. It'll take all night before her circuits are dead. We'll send her for dismantling in the morning.'

Spike showed no emotion as she listened to this. Presumably she has no emotion to show.

'All right,' said Manfred. 'We might want to film the last few flickers for the human content.'

'I'll come back later,' I said.

'No, you won't,' said Manfred. 'You're done here.'

Suddenly he stood still, listening to his Inner Voice from Central Command. He pointed at the Wall2WallTV and zapped it live. His face was excited. 'They've got the Competition Countdown Winners!'

'What winners? What competition?' I said.

Manfred looked at me the way you look at a pre-packed sandwich you don't want to eat. 'Billie – are you always out of touch with real life or do I misjudge you?'

'Manfred, I have been out all day dealing with paedophiles and parking meters – I haven't got time for real life. Just tell me what's happening!'

Spike leaned forward. 'MORE-*Life* has sponsored a celebrity promotional trip to Planet Blue.'

Red carpet, spinning lights, big band, girls in bikinis throwing blow-up beach balls of Planet Blue into the audience. Down the lit-up centre-aisle crucifix comes Martin Moody, TV host to the stars. The audience goes wild. Moody Media is mega.

'He is such a performer!' says Manfred. 'So real!'

Martin Moody lifts up his hands like a politician –

There were two questions . . . DRUM ROLL.

There were two answers . . . DRUM ROLL.

WHAT IS THE NAME OF THE NEW PLANET?

WHAT DOES THE NEW PLANET WEIGH?

TIE BREAKER: If YOU were in charge of Planet Blue, what would you do first? Tell us and Win!

WIN! And you could be one of the first to visit the new world for the weekend! Sponsored by MORE-*Life*, on-line on-land, the global company working for YOU.

Martin welcomes his first live guest. A thick-set man in blue jeans and a white T-shirt blows kisses at the audience. The audience cheers. Martin Moody steps forward – '*Let's welcome Derek!*'

All right, Martin? My name's Derek and I'm a cab driver, but my hobby is fuckin' parrots.

And what do the parrots think of that, Derek? (Audience laughter.)

Aw, Martin, you know what I'm talking about! (*Laughter.*) I breed 'em, old-fashioned style – no cloning, just let 'em get on wiv it. I got a hundred and fifty, used to have three hundred and fifty. All in a fuckin' aviary on the side of the front room so the wife can watch 'em while I'm out workin'. There won't be no cabs on Planet Blue, not to start wiv anyway, so I'm gettin' my own fuckin' parrot business goin', before they start all that fuckin' licence-exotic-fuckin'-pet rubbish. I'm sayin', No red tape on Planet Blue! (Audience: *Go for it, Derek . . . Waves, leaves.*)

MM comes forward: *Vote Derek from Brighton if you say no red tape on Planet Blue.* (Laughter.) *Next guest, please!*

Martin! (*Kiss, kiss.*) My name is Kingdom Come, and I have my own fashion label – I really think we could get some cool clothes going on Planet Blue.

You said in your tie-breaker that we need to start with retail?

That's right. Shopping centres, people – it's holistic. That's why we call the malls shopping centres.

I never knew that . . .

Yeah, Martin, that's why. (*Nods wisely.*) If people buy a brand they can trust, they feel better about themselves.

(Audience: *That's right!*) The first thing we gotta do on Planet Blue is get some reliable merchandise out there! I can do that – own-label Planet Blue clothes! (*Waves, bows.*)

Vote Kingdom Come if you want the centred shopping experience. Next guest, please.

Martin, I can't believe I'm really here and not dreaming! My name is Mary McMurphy – Pink for short – and I'm a celebrity-chaser, so I'd like to think that on Planet Blue I can get a start-up going – y'know, a celebrity on-line type of thing? I mean, the stars are, well, they're stars, aren't they, like you see in the sky? It's a cute connection. (*Audience claps.*)

But, Pink, there won't be any celebrities on Planet Blue at first.

Y'know, that's why we'll need an on-line presence – it'll be like a strong connection with where we've come from. People need strong connections. (*Audience yaps approval.*)

Vote Pink McMurphy for that celebrity connection – don't fall over, Pink. Next guest, please.

Hello there, Martin. (*Double handshake.*) My name is Tim and I think that the very first thing we need to get right on Planet Blue, yes, the first and very, is the parking – I'm a traffic-management consultant . . .

Don't be modest, Tim – you're a bit of a guru, aren't you?

I have my own radio show, Martin – *Prime Time Parking* (*cheering*) – where listeners can phone in with news of spaces and places, spots and slots. Without a doubt, parking is the number-one issue facing the world today – not for politicians, I admit, but for ordinary people like you and me. The first thing on our minds when we wake up is, Where am I going to park without getting a ticket? (*Audience stomps and drums.*)

Vote Tim if you want your own parking space on Planet Blue. Next guest.

My name is Nomad, and I represent all the people who don't know why we're here. (*Audience silence.*)

So, Nomad, if you don't know why you're here, why have you come? (*Audience laughter.*)

I'm frightened that the world is ending. I don't want to die.

Thanks, Nomad, thanks for your views. (Nomad is escorted offstage.) *I think we had a little hiccup there — but let's move on. Celine . . .*

Hi! HiHiHi! MynameisCeline. IrunaSpeedDatingService. Ispeakfast. It'sahabitofthejob. TheremightbepeopleonPlanetBlue (*cough*) needingtomeetYOU. (*Applause, laughter.*)

Celine, you said that we should get a dating service going as soon as we can — before we get any homes or roads or even retail — is that right?

'SrightMartin! Lovecomesfirst! (*Audience whoops.*)

Vote Celine if you think that love comes first . . .

Manfred switched the wall-screen blank. 'Brilliant promotion. That will push the whole relocation to a new level.'

'I thought we were starting with a Science Station?'

'We are — but who cares about that? We need real people to keep the interest going. Scientists aren't interesting.'

'Thanks.'

'It's not personal.'

So when is this next mission, complete with Reality TV winner?'

'Soon. No thanks to the attempted sabotage — but I suppose you don't know about that either? The Resistance is back.'

'Perhaps it never went away.'

Manfred said nothing for a moment. Then he said, 'Perhaps knowledge is selective – what we know, what we don't know. What we say we don't know.'

'Billie . . .' It was Spike interrupting. 'Thank you for the interview.'

She was speaking to break the moment. I smiled at her; she nodded.

Manfred got up and motioned me towards the door. We walked in silence through the corridors. As we stood waiting for the elevator, he said, 'Billie, take a few days' holiday. I would if I were you.'

'Are you trying to tell me something?'

'This is a sensitive time. If anything goes wrong, I don't want it to go wrong from my department.'

'Are you saying that I am the Wrong that should go?'

'I'm saying take a few days' holiday.'

The elevator doors opened. GOING UP. Manfred stepped inside. The doors closed.

I waited. LIGHT. PING. GOING DOWN.

On the streets everyone was wearing their pollution filters. Everyone had the glassy-eyed, good-looking look that is normal nowadays. Even in an air-mask people are concerned to look good. The State gives out masks on demand, but the smart people have their own designer versions.

There was a woman in front of me, fumbling with her mask, coughing. I went to help her, and she grabbed my hand, 'Getting old,' she said, and I wondered if I had misheard because we don't use those words any more. We don't need to use them: they are irrelevant to our experience.

'Getting old,' she said again. Then she pulled off her

mask. Her eyes were bright and glittering, but her face was lined, worn, weathered, battered, purple-veined and liver-spotted, with a slot for a mouth, garishly coated with red lipstick.

I recoiled. I had never seen a living person look like this. I had seen archive footage of how we used to age, and I had seen some of the results of medical experiments, but in front of me, now, was a thing with skin like a lizard's, like a stand-up handbag.

'I am what you will become,' she said. 'I know you haven't been Fixed.'

'You don't know anything!' I said, angry, frightened.

She laughed. 'Look at me. When I was your age, was I planning to wind up like this? No. I was political, like you. I thought we should take a stand, like you. And for the last twenty years I have only been able to go out on pollution days so that no one can see my face. If you saw my body, you'd throw up.'

She pulled back the sleeve of her coat. Her arm was bones and stretched flesh – brown, thin skin pulled over bluish, visible tendons. I looked away. One of the smart buildings was flashing one of the usual feel-good advertisements sponsored by MORE-*Life*. Kids, their parents and grandparents, all identically handsome, wearing the same dirt-free nano-clothes, picnicking in the State Park – *Best Days of Your Life – For as Long as Your Life*.

The old woman was laughing. She had no teeth.

I forced myself to look at her calmly. 'Why are you talking to me like this?'

'They know about you.'

'Who knows about me?'

'They know you faked your records.'

'That's not true!'

45

'I'm telling you now. They know who you are.'

The woman pulled down her full-face mask and moved slowly away.

I stood quite still, like an animal that fears a predator. The red dust was blowing through the empty street.

As I stood, not knowing what to do, my phone started flashing Manfred's code. I didn't want to speak to him, but he can tell via satellite recognition exactly where I am. I have a personal co-ordinate, like everyone else, and anyone with the access code can access me, whether or not I would prefer to hide.

I take his call. His voice is rammed with anger. 'The Robo *sapiens* has escaped!'

'She's not a Great Ape. What do you mean, escaped?'

'You heard me. Did she give you any clues?'

'No, of course not. I thought you were dismantling her.'

'The techies went for a break, and when they came back she'd disappeared. She might contact you.'

'She won't contact me – why would she contact me?'

'Her data shows that she has formed a connection with you.'

'Well, I haven't formed a connection with her. Manfred, I do not know what has happened to Spike.'

'If she comes to you –'

'She won't come to me – she doesn't know where to find me. She couldn't access my data-chip while she was draining, she told me that herself.'

There is a pause. He knows this is true. He had a theory, now he's not sure. I take my chance. 'She'll go to the Border. She must be defecting.'

'Robots can't defect. They aren't made to think for themselves.'

'This one was.'

Another pause. 'The Border? You think so? Are you telling me something?'

'I'm not telling you anything, Manfred. I have nothing to tell.'

As the phone clicked off I felt calm again, with the calm of knowing that whatever happened next, in some strange way, I'd had to come to this place. A point of no return. This place . . . real and imaginary. Actual and about to be.

I drove home along the sea road. The shining white towers of the city to the left of me were just beginning to soften, as they do every night, in response to the evening light.

On my right, the ocean front, strong and straight and beautiful, pulled the city towards it, as if this was our only dream, and we would never wake up but we would walk under the palm trees and up through the beautiful buildings, hand in hand, free and new.

In truth the city sprawls back and back, blank and bored, but here, where it is how it was meant to be, it feels possible and true.

And it feels like it will go on for ever.

I can't believe that we have reached the end of everything. The red dust is frightening. The carbon dioxide is real. Water is expensive. Bio-tech has created as many problems as it has fixed, but, but, we're here, we're alive, we're the human race, we have survived wars and terrorism and scarcity and global famine, and we have made it back from the brink, not once but many times. History is not a suicide note – it is a record of our survival.

Look, the sun is setting on the level bar of the ocean, and whatever I say, whatever I feel, this is home, and I am going home.

I pulled off the road to the bottom of the track that leads to the farm.

On my left is the broad, active stream with watercress growing in the fast part, and flag iris on the bank, and a willow bending over the water, and a foam of frog spawn, and a moorhen sailing the current.

The track rises steeply. It's getting dark. Ahead of me is the compact stone house, water-barrel by the front door, apple tree at the gate. *Go in*, I say to myself, *go in*.

And I slept that night, long and deep, like someone who does not dream because she is dreaming already.

Morning. The next day.

The man at the door had a face like a pickaxe. His job was to make a big hole in my life. 'Your name Crusoe?'

'I'm the one.'

'This place Cast Out Farm?'

'No, it's the Library of Congress.'

Sensing trouble – that is, daring to taunt an Enforcement Officer – the moribund CanCop riding the back of the bike jerked to life.

'Why d'you bring the soup tin with you? There's only me here – what's the problem?'

The Enforcement guy said nothing. His eyes ran over the cut-stone house with its big wide dented doors and its moss-slated roof. My dog Rufus was growling in his spot by the front gate. The horses in the field looked up from their grazing. It was an ordinary day, unlike any other. 'Might be all kinds of types here,' he said.

The CanCop got off the bike and started taking snaps of the place with his built-in head camera.

'This place isn't a tourist attraction,' I said. 'It's private land. Tell the tin monkey to behave itself.'

The Arm of the Law ignored me. 'This is your Court Order.' He flicked the screen on the windshield of his HoverBike, and there were all my details: name, address, age, occupation, money owed, money owed, money, money.

'I don't owe this money.'

'You gotta tell that to the Court.'

'You're a human being, aren't you?'

'Mostly.' He shuffled on the seat of the bike. He had refit legs, the kind that never get tired of chasing criminals, like me.

'I wasn't talking about your legs. Your brain is human. Your heart is human. All of these fines have been contested and cleared. Every single one.'

He flicked through the notes on his screen. His notes are not words, they are numbers. 'Coder says all fines still outstanding.'

'How much do I owe?'

'Says here three million dollars.'

'But these are parking fines!'

'That's right. One year's worth of parking fines, add Orders, add Enforcement, add costs of Contesting, add Interest. That's right, dollars three million.'

'Just a minute – if there are Contesting costs there, then the Coder knows I have contested. There is just one single massive error – I know I've been systematically cleared, and the Coder doesn't. This isn't a judgement, it's a software problem.'

'Nothing I can do about it. I don't make the rules.'

49

(Don't you want to kill every moron who says that?)

I tried to be patient. I tried a new line. 'You work for Enforcement, right?'

He nodded. They like simple sentences.

'OK, and I work for Enhancement. Now, I can't enhance anybody's life unless I can get into their house and see what the problem is. I can't get into the house unless I can park outside, which is why Enhancement Officers – me – have Exemption Permits, like Enforcement Officers – you.'

'Permits aren't my job.'

'Here is my permit.'

In answer, he pushed back his bike and jabbed a code on to his windshield. 'I'm putting here that you refuse the Judgement.'

'I have been trying for one whole year to speak to a human being in Enforcement. I want a human being to look at my permit and tell me why it is not valid, although it is active and in date, and I want a human being to tell me why I owe the Central Power three million dollars.'

He was jabbing his Coder again.

'What are you doing now?' I said.

'I am coding your response.'

'Don't code my response! Give me the name of someone I can talk to.'

'Your number is 116SS,' he said. 'I've sent it to your screen and I've sent it back to base. You got one week to pay up or we take the farm.'

Rufus was howling. 'You should take him in and get him Fixed,' said Pickaxe.

'He's a real dog – even his legs are real. I can't get him Fixed. He's a real dog.'

50

Pickaxe showed his first flicker of interest. 'No kidding? Like the ones at the Zooeum?'

'Yeah, he's a real-life out-of-date animal. He breeds, he barks, he dies.'

'I got a Robo-collie. He's a real nice round-up dog. Very affectionate. I keep his bark-button switched off.'

Rufus was barking and baring his teeth. The CanCop lumbered over to kick him. Without thinking, I picked up a bucket of water from the back step and threw it right over his clanking can of a body.

It worked. The thing short-circuited and stopped dead.

'Now you're sure in trouble,' said the Lone Ranger. 'CanCops are protected by the State.'

'Unlike people,' I said, my hand trembling on the dog's head. 'Now put him on your bike and get lost.'

High Noon looked down at Rufus again. 'Dog like that could be classified as dangerous.'

'Every animal on this farm has a licence. The farm has a licence.'

'Central Power's thinking of revoking those licences, you know that?'

'They can't. The licences are for the life of the farm.'

'But what's the life of the farm?' He paused and scraped the heel of his boot in the dust of the track. 'Come to talk about it, what's life?'

This man is not a philosopher, I thought. What's he saying to me?

He slung the CanCop over the back of the HoverBike, and set off down the track. There he goes, cut to fit, machine-made, State-owned, low-maintenance, dream-free, inoculated against doubt. Life is so simple when you're just doing your job.

I have to stop shaking.

Back inside the house, on the plasma wall, the number was there, 116SS, and next to it, ticking down in digital red, the number of days, hours, minutes, seconds I had left before I had to quit.

I threw an egg at the wall. 'Oh!' said the wall, complainingly, no need for VI-O-LENCE.' It separates the syllables because its computer box is an old model, like one of those antique speaking clocks. 'I do not CH-OO-SE what appears on the wall.'

'They'll be knocking you down soon – we're being evicted.'

The wall was silent.

It was late at night, and I was sitting by my fire, burning applewood in the hearth, when I heard footsteps walking slowly towards the back door. Rufus growled. I picked up a heavy bottle and cautiously went forward. 'Who's there?' I said, trying to keep my voice firm.

'Manfred.'

I opened the door. Manfred was standing outside, bending down, undoing his canvas sneakers. 'Cow-shit,' he said.

I took them from his outstretched hand and held open the door. 'If you had the bio-dome code, why did you come via the cow-shit?'

'This place is being watched. I came in the back way, using the Museum Services Access Code.'

He stepped in, looking round at the farmhouse table and the messy real food on it: a brown loaf, butter, eggs in a bowl.

'Do you want something to eat?' I said.

'I'm a Natural Nutrition man,' he said, meaning he eats

only the most expensive synthetics, protein- and mineral-balanced for optimum health.

I took his sneakers to the sink and started swilling off the cow-shit. 'I had Enforcement round today,' I said. 'Parking fines.'

'That's an excuse,' he said. 'Enforcement wants to arrest you. I expect you know why.'

I didn't answer him. 'If you're looking for your robot, she isn't here.'

'I know that.'

'What else do you know? Or think you know?'

He pulled out a chair. 'Billie, I'm going to call you in the morning and offer you a chance to make the trip to Planet Blue with Moody Media. They were very impressed by your One Minute Special. They need an expert who can communicate. They don't want a scientist-type.'

'I am a scientist-type.'

'You're hiding Unknowns.'

I dropped his shoes into the sink. I didn't look at him. 'Don't talk rubb –'

Manfred grabbed my arm with surprising strength. He held my left forearm up to the light. There was a short, neat scar.

'That was where you had your tagger removed. Your data-chip has been reprocessed.'

'I was acquitted.'

'You were tagged pending further evidence.'

'There was no case against me.'

'Soon you will be under arrest. The parking fines have been cooked up to get you out of here without looking like a martyr. Once Enforcement have got hold of you, even if you're innocent, and I don't believe you are – no, don't argue, listen, even if you're Snow White – it will take you years to prove it.'

'So what are you saying?'

'I'm saying that you're a problem. Enforcement just wants you arrested because when they tried to bring a case against you three years ago – for acts of Terrorism against the State that included aiding, abetting and hiding Unknowns, you got away with it. They don't forgive and they don't forget.'

'I didn't get away with anything. I was tried and acquitted. I was not hiding Unknowns then, and I am not hiding them now.'

'And I am the Man in the Moon. Listen to me, Billie. I've had the go-ahead from the top – the very top – to offer you this one chance to leave quietly. This isn't the time for a big fuss about your arrest. We don't want any crap-headed liberals arguing over admissible evidence. Right now, you are an embarrassment. You're more trouble than you're worth. You bucked the system. That's not allowed. Either we get you this time – or you go. For reasons of the moment, we'd prefer you to go.'

'We?'

'Let's say I'm more than my day-job.'

'An informer?'

'I believe in the system. You don't.'

'No, I don't. It's repressive, corrosive and anti-democratic.'

'Then you'll be very happy on Planet Blue. There is no system.'

'And what happens when I come back?'

He didn't answer.

I started drying his shoes on a towel. 'Are they really coming for me, Manfred?'

'Yes.'

'What will happen to the farm?'

'It's legally yours – unless, of course, you can't clear your parking fines, and then the State may take it in lieu of payment.'

'You mean I'm going to lose the farm whatever happens?'

'No, you could claim the whole parking thing is a fabrication against you – which it is – and then Enforcement will ask to reopen your previous failed conviction on the grounds of new evidence from one of the Unknowns captured in the Space Compound.'

'There is no new evidence against me. There is no old evidence against me. There are no parking fines.'

I handed Manfred his shoes. He put them on. 'Play it how you like, Billie. It's over to you now. This meeting between us never happened. I have witnesses to say exactly where I am tonight, and it isn't here. In the morning I will call you and offer you the chance to travel to Planet Blue. The call will be recorded.'

He was gone.

I watched his dark shape disappear across the fields. I went inside and looked around me. Is this how easy it is to lose everything?

Nightstream – and, hurtling towards me, another day.

Answer the phone, Billie. Answer the phone.

Chance of a lifetime – new start – brave new world – wipe the slate clean – blue-sky moment – open the box – never too late – historic opportunity – commemorative plaque/T-shirt/travel mug/bath towel. Fifteen minutes of fame –

live for ever – immortalized in space – happy few – happy ever after – don't look back – no regrets – something to tell the grandchildren – giant leap for mankind.

Tripped over on the red carpet, she did, winner of the MORE-*Life* Competition, dazzled by celebrity, Pink McMurphy aboard the Starship *Resolution*: 'Y'know, this is the best day of my en-tire life.' It wasn't that she was going to Planet Blue, it was that Little Señorita would be cutting the tape, smashing the bottle, waving the blast-off flag and kissing the lucky winner on both cheeks.

Cheers, tears, saxophones, catwalk celebrities, webcam, blog, helicopters, live coverage, pom-poms, confetti, clock, countdown, blast-off. Yes!

We were lining the windows of the Ship, we were watching the crowds wave and shout. The band was faint and far away. The silver confetti was falling back to the ground. We were pushing out of the hazy carbon blanket that lies above Orbus. It was as though we had left a harbour at night, and in fog, and then, as we waited on deck, listening for the last muffled bell of land, the sun rose and we set sail through the clean emptiness of another chance.

Captain Handsome was a space privateer – don't use the word 'pirate'. He was a swashbuckling freelance predator with semi-official sanction. Where there was work to be done that couldn't be seen to be done, enter Handsome.

Handsome had his own ship: a light, fast, solar-sailed craft that he used to traffic booty for rich collectors. The trade in other worlds was like any other, but still romantic. Handsome was part-swagger, part-alchemist. He had girls and gold, but he had a poetic side too. He had bargained with the dead, he said, and brought back more than trophies: his rocks and minerals in their sealed cases, his hostile atmospheres, captured in jars and swirling like genies, were something more than money could buy – they were the runes of other lives, silent and mysterious, clues that might be followed one day, and lead to . . .

'There are mountains so high you can't see to the top, and inland lakes, locked and closed, far from any water source but agitated beneath the surface by dark shapes.

'There are valleys that lead to the bottom of the world, so it seems, but what world is that? The universe has no sides, no end, can't be mapped. Enough to make a man talk about God, make a man superstitious and worship an idol. The science never gets as far as the strangeness. The more sophisticated my equipment, the stranger the worlds it detects. I sometimes think I'm sailing through a vast thought.'

Handsome had tracked the official space mission to Planet Blue. In the pay of MORE-*Futures* he had been trophy-hunting the Jurassic equivalent of Big Game. Now he was playing for much higher stakes.

'What use is a planet that belongs to the dinosaurs? For the first time in my career I find myself with State approval. Not that I haven't worked for the State before, you understand, but let's say it was kept quiet. This is a Central Power Mission. Flags, bells, whistles. Yes, I am travelling for the President. My job is to get rid of the dinosaurs – and when I do, we're going back to a fairytale. I will defeat the dragon and be offered the kingdom.'

'You will own Planet Blue?' I said, incredulous – this sounded like good going, even for a pirate.

'The Central Power will own Planet Blue. I will take my share, a vast virgin country bounded by rivers. Dragon, kingdom and . . . princess . . .'

'Who's your princess?' I asked.

'You've met her. You could say she's your sponsor.'

And Spike came smiling across the ship and kissed Handsome. 'Hello, Billie,' she said.

'I thought I was the one who was supposed to be helping you escape.'

'As it turned out, there was no need . . .'

'I organized that part,' said Handsome. 'I refused to leave without her.'

'And then we heard you were coming aboard.'

'It was a little bit unexpected.'

'Join the party,' said Handsome, which was a mistake as Pink McMurphy was sliding by, and to her the word 'party' was the same as the word 'drink' – lots of it.

Handsome took his cue and brought out the champagne, fizzing the Jeroboam, and throwing it like liquid rope into bollard-shaped glasses. 'To Planet Blue,' he said, raising his glass, and there on the diode screen was the picture of our new world, and underneath:

She is all States, all Princes I . . .

'And to you,' he said to Spike.

'Isn't she a robot?' said Pink, in an unusual moment of moral questioning.

Just then my luggage started to bark.

'What's in the bag?' asked Handsome – the kind of man who was used to barking bags.

'Did you think I was going to leave my dog behind?'

'Can't leave behind what you love,' said Handsome, but I didn't answer that.

★

Pink McMurphy, in her kitten heels, was looking around the main deck in some confusion. 'What's all this writing stuff?' she said.

– *I was born in the year 1632, in the city of York, of a good family, tho' not of that country . . .*

'It's a shipwreck story,' said Handsome. 'The men like it.'

'Are these things books?' asked Pink, picking a crumbling volume off the shelf. 'That's cute. I never seen one of these.'

'We were flying in a strange part of the sky,' said Handsome, 'and we thought we'd hit a meteorite shower, ship spinning like a windsock in a gale. I took a three-hundred-and-sixty-degree shot of the ship, and I saw that what we were flying through was a bookstorm – encyclopedias, dictionaries, a Uniform Edition of the Romantic poets, the complete works of Shakespeare.'

'Yeah, I heard of him,' said Pink, nodding.

'Scott, Defoe. We netted as much as we could – some were just loose lost pages and those I glued on the walls. This one is my favourite – I read it again and again.' He lifted down a battered eighteenth-century edition of Captain Cook's *Journals*. 'The record of where he sailed – Tahiti, New Zealand, Brazil. I feel I know him. I feel he would understand what we're trying to do now. You should read it – here.' He passed me the book – I opened it at random:

March 1774. We plied to windward in order to get into a Bay which appeared on the South East side of the island, but night put a stop to our endeavours.

'Where did these books come from?' I asked, but Handsome just shook his head.

'A repeating world – same old story.'

'What do you mean?'

'You'll hear enough of my theories later,' he said. 'Spike doesn't swallow a word of it.' He paused. 'I taught the crew to read.'

'Handsome is old-fashioned,' said Spike. 'He believes in reading and breeding.'

'Not me,' said Pink. 'I like downloads and womb-free.'

There was a whistle from above, and Handsome was called away to balance the solar sails. I took my chance. 'Spike, why is Handsome on this mission, and not the Central Power Space Force?'

'Handsome believes he has found a way to solve the problem that doesn't involve poison or nuclear pollution. The planet is pristine . . .'

'I was told they're already selling real estate,' said Pink. 'Dinosaurs will depress the house prices.'

'We underestimated the threat,' said Spike. 'Dinosaurs are an early evolutionary species, human beings are a late evolutionary species. We can't cohabit.'

'Y'know, I think that's what's wrong with my marriage,' said Pink.

'He's looking for an asteroid,' said Spike. 'He's going to use a gravity charge to deflect its course to collide with Planet Blue.'

Handsome's swashbuckling science was beyond me; it seemed like a pretty dim idea to use space like a bowling alley to knock out the dinosaurs.

'That's not what he has in mind,' said Spike. 'The asteroid won't kill the dinosaurs directly, but indirectly. He's going to create a duststorm of a very particular kind . . .'

★

I looked at her. Green eyes, dark hair, olive skin. Perfect because she had been designed perfect. Low, gentle voice, intelligent face. If she had been human . . .

I wish she wouldn't read my mind.

It was suppertime. The crew sat round a long table facing plates the size of satellite dishes, spooning meat and vegetables from enormous steaming pans and helping each other to wine from a barrel. They were telling stories, the way all shipcrew tell stories.

There's a planet they call Medusa. It's made of rock all right, but the rock has sharded and split so many times that there's nothing solid — just strands of rock, splintered out from the surface like thick plaits of hair. Like snakes. When the sky-winds blow, the rock-strands move, and something about the wind through them makes them sing. It's as if a head is turned away from you, always turned away, and singing through the darkness, dark and lonely, never see her face.

There's a planet called Morpheus. Its atmosphere is dense and heavy, like walking in heat after rain. Anything that flies into its orbit never comes out again. You can see in there the litter of spacecraft and tiny asteroids, and there's a man in a helmet, arms out, drifting through eternity. Get caught there, and you hang for ever, never to wake, an endless dream. The cloud-gas is a narcotic. It's a part of space that sleeps, like a castle in a wood, like an enchantment that missed the magic word. No time, no motion, a world held in waiting.

There's a planet called Echo. It doesn't exist. It's like those ghost-ships at sea, the sails worn through and the deck empty. It comes on the radar, you fly towards it, there's nothing there. Our crew were outside, repairing the craft, and we saw it moving at speed right at us. It passed straight through the ship and through our bodies, and the strange thing that happened was the bleach. It bleached our clothes and hair, and men that had black beards had white. Then it was gone, echoing in another part of the starry sky, always, 'here' and 'here' and 'here', but nowhere. Some call it Hope.

Chanc'd upon, spied through a glass darkly, strapped to a barrel of rum, shipwreck, a Bible Compass, a giant fish led us there, a storm whirled us to this isle. In the wilderness of space, we found . . .

We found a planet, and it was white like a shroud. The planet was wrapped in its own death. We lowered ourselves through mists like mountains, cragged, formed, shaped, but not solid. Put out your hand and you put it through a ghost. Every solid thing had turned to thick vapour.

We dropped through winds that could not shift the clouds until we reached a land where the air – if it was air – was like paste. We would soon have made porridge out of our lungs if we had breathed it, and burning porridge too, for the place, as white and cold as death, is as hot as rage. The planet is a raging death.

Or it is a thing that has been killed and rages to be dead.

There were forests there – each leafless trunk brittle as charcoal, but not black, white. White weapons in blasted rows, as though some ancient army had rested its spears and never returned.

We moved slant-wise though the blasted spears that dwarfed us. Our boots sank into the white, crumbled rock of the planet's surface. Like cinders it was, cinders burned so hot that every blackness had been bleached out of them. Dig a spadeful, and there was nothing solid beneath. Vapour, crumbled rock, and the trees riddled through like white honeycomb, like some desperate thing had fought for a last hiding-place, and not found it.

There had been oceans on the white planet. We found a sea-floor, ridged and scooped, and shells as brittle as promises, and bones cracked like hope. White, everything white, but not the white of a morning when the sun will pour through it, nor the white of a clean cloth; not the white of a cheese where you can smell the green of the grass that fed the goat, nor the white of a hand that you love.

There is a white that contains all the colours of the world but this white was its mockery. This was the white at the end of the world when nothing is left, not the past, not the present and, most fearful of all, not the future. There was no future in this bleached and boiled place. Nothing, not wild, not strange, not tiny, not vile, no good thing, no bad, could begin life again here. The world was a white-out. The experiment was done.

We found the ruins of a city, and the ruin of a road that ran to it. A proud place this had been, once upon a time, once upon a time like the words in a fairytale. The ruins of a city, and it might have been sitting under the sea, for the pressure on the surface of this planet is as great as that half a mile under the sea. The weight of this world is its own despair.

Without armour of a kind, anyone would be crushed. Without oxygen, no one here can breathe at all. Without fireproof clothing, you would be charred as the rest of what was once life.

And yet there was once life here, naked and free and optimistic.

We walked through the sunken city, and into the Crypt of the planet, and there we found a thing that amazed us. Like an elephant's graveyard, the Crypt was stacked with the carcasses of planes and cars that continually melted in the intense heat and then re-formed into their old shapes, or shapes more bizarre, as the cars grew wings, and the planes compressed into wheelless boxes with upturned tails.

Such heat without fire is hard to imagine, but this was the inferno, where a civilization has taken its sacrifices and piled them to some eyeless god, but too late. The sacrifice was not accepted. The planet burned.

The men cheered and banged the table, and Rufus barked.

'Is that a true story?' I said.

'Stories are always true,' said Handsome. 'It's the facts that mislead.'

Later, when the men had eaten, and we were alone, I spoke to Spike about the white planet. She pulled up some images from her database. There it was, bright as life, radiating the sky. How could it be dead?

She said, 'The strange thing about Planet White is that it shares the sun of Planet Blue. When we first found it we thought it would be viable for us, but investigation shows that life flourished there light years away from now, and that life was destroyed, or that life destroyed itself, which seems the only possible explanation. It is too near the sun now, that is true, and it has an atmosphere that is ninety-seven per cent carbon dioxide. It has become a greenhouse planet, but a cruel one, sheltering nothing. It no longer has water, though it is likely that water was once abundant.'

'And what about the Crypt?'

'I have seen the images. Call it a traveller's tale.'

'Is it a traveller's tale?'

She shrugged. 'Imagine it – walking through the whited-out world, fitted deep inside a thermal compression suit, like diving gear but built to withstand both pressure and intolerable heat. The petrified forest is there – carbonized tree remains, held in the heat, we don't know how, like a memory.

'And then there are oceanic indicators, yes, and then

there is what might have been a city, yes, and what might have been a road, yes, but as unfathomable as those boiling explosions that form our own undersea worlds. And there is what those who have seen it call the Crypt.

'It is a landfill site, thousands of miles deep, and high, and filled with something that does not disappear, though it should. Those who have seen it are terrified and will swear that what they see are the twisted, destroyed shapes of planes and cars, more than could be counted, molten but not melted.'

'What else could it be?'

'A mirage. The heat is searing. White-hot clouds cover everything. For a moment, the clouds part. A man sees something he thinks he recognizes from another life. Does he recognize it or does he invent it?'

'What do you think?'

'I do not know.'

'But what do you think?'

'I'll tell you what I think,' said Captain Handsome, coming into the room and throwing himself on the bench, his head in Spike's lap, 'and I'll tell it the way any sailor would – through a story, an old old story this one, handed down from the ships to the space-ships.'

Handsome said:

There was a young man with a hot temper. He was not all bad, but he was reckless, and he drank more than he should, and spent more than he could, and gave a ring to more women than one, and gambled himself into a corner so tight an ant couldn't turn round in it. One night, in despair, and desperate with worry, he got into a fight outside a bar, and killed a man.

Mad with fear and remorse, for he was more hot-tempered than wicked, and stupid when he could have been wise, he locked himself into his filthy bare attic room and took the revolver that had killed his enemy, loaded it, cocked it and prepared to blast himself to pieces.

In the few moments before he pulled the trigger, he said, 'If I had known that all that I have done would bring me to this, I would have led a very different life. If I could live my life again, I would not be here, with the trigger in my hand and the barrel at my head.'

His good angel was sitting by him and, feeling pity for the young man, the angel flew to Heaven and interceded on his behalf.

Then in all his six-winged glory, the angel appeared before the terrified boy, and granted him his wish. 'In full knowledge of what you have become, go back and begin again.'

And suddenly, the young man had another chance.

For a time, all went well. He was sober, upright, true, thrifty. Then one night he passed a bar, and it seemed familiar to him, and he went in and gambled all he had, and he met a woman and told her he had no wife, and he stole from his employer, and spent all he could.

And his debts mounted with his despair, and he decided to gamble everything on one last throw of the dice. This time, as the wheel spun and slowed, his chance would be on the black, not the red. This time, he would win.

The ball fell in the fateful place, as it must.

The young man had lost.

He ran outside, but the men followed him, and in a brawl with the bar owner, he shot him dead, and found himself alone and hunted in a filthy attic room.

He took out his revolver. He primed it. He said, 'If I'd known that I could do such a thing again, I would never have risked it.

I would have lived a different life. If I had known where my actions would lead me . . .'

And his angel came, and sat by him, and took pity on him once again, and interceded for him, and . . .

And years passed, and the young man was doing well until he came to a bar that seemed familiar to him . . .

Bullets, revolver, attic, angel, begin again. Bar, bullets, revolver, attic, angel, begin again . . . angel, bar, ball, bullets . . .

Handsome sat up, leaning on one arm. 'The only intelligent life in the Universe. The only *life* in the Universe. Solitary, privileged, spinning alone on our red planet, the strangest serendipity of chance and good luck? Look out of the window. These burned-out rocks aren't all accidents of space. Humans or humanoids, or bionoids or mutants or ETS, who can say? but some life-form, capable like ours of developing, and, like all things that are capable of development, capable of destruction too.'

'Are you saying that the white planet . . .'

'Was where we used to live.'

'There is no evidence for that,' said Spike.

'What do you want to find? A talking head buried in the sand?'

Spike said, 'There is only evidence that life in some form existed at some time on planets other than our own, including, but not exclusively, the white planet.'

'The white planet was a world like ours,' said Handsome, 'far, far advanced. We were still evolving out of the soup when the white planet had six-lane highways and space missions. It was definitely a living, breathing, working planet, with water and resources, cooked to cinders by CO_2. They couldn't control their gases. Certainly the planet was heating up anyway, but the humans, or whatever they were, massively miscalculated, and pumped so much CO_2 into the air that they caused irreversible warming. The rest is history.'

'Whose history?'

'Looking more and more like ours, don't you think?' said Handsome. 'Anyway, I like the colour co-ordination – a dead white planet, a dying red planet, and Planet Blue out there, just starting up.'

'Our planet . . .'

'Is red,' said Handsome. 'That red-dust stuff?'

'Is sand,' said Spike.

'Yes, it is sand, but it is not just desert sand. The desert advances every year, but the duststorms are not just sand, they are the guts of the fucking planet. It's iron ore in there.'

'There is no evidence for that,' said Spike.

'Iron ore? Of course there is.'

'No evidence that we are gutting Orbus.'

'Well, I don't know what you call it, but a planet that has collapsing ice-caps, encroaching desert, no virgin forest and no eco-species left reads like gutted to me. The place is just throwing up and, I tell you, it's not the first time. My theory is that life on Orbus began as escaping life from the white planet – and the white planet began as escaping life from . . . who knows where?'

Pink was visibly moved by the story. 'Y'know, it would make a great movie. It has a human feel.'

Ignoring the cinematic possibilities of global disaster on a galactic scale, I said, 'But it's so depressing if we keep making the same mistakes again and again . . .'

Pink was sympathetic. 'I know what you mean – every time we fall in love.'

'I wasn't thinking personal,' I said.

'What's the difference?' she said. 'Women are just planets that attract the wrong species.'

'It might be more complex than that,' said Spike.

'They use us up, wear us out, then cast us off for a younger model so that they can do it all again.'

'But, Pink, you are the younger model. Genetic Fixing changed all that,' I said.

'It didn't work, though, did it? Y'know what I mean?'

'Women always bring it back to the personal,' said Handsome. 'It's why you can't be world leaders.'

'And men never do,' I said, 'which is why we end up with no world left to lead.'

He held up his hands. 'I'm beaten. I'll leave you ladies to destroy what's left of the male sex.' He bent over and kissed Spike.

'Isn't she a robot?' asked Pink, who was nothing if not her own repeating history.

'The champagne's in the cooler,' said Handsome, and left.

Pink sighed. 'He's so strong, so romantic. He's like a hero from the Discovery Channel. I just don't understand why he's in love with a robot – no offence intended to you, Spike, I'm not prejudiced or anything, it's not your fault that you're a robot – I mean, you never had any say in it, did you? One minute you were a pile of wires, and the next thing you know you're having an affair.'

'I don't love Handsome,' said Spike.

'Well, of course not – y'know, like I said, you're a robot.'

'That isn't why I don't love him,' said Spike, but Pink wasn't listening.

'What about you, Billie?' she said. 'What's your story? Now that we're in space we can say what we like. I feel much better since we left Orbus – I think maybe I was allergic to gravity. It's kind of flattening.'

Spike looked at me. I shrugged. 'There was someone. It didn't work out. If I'm truthful I would say that it's never worked out. Almost, nearly, but not quite. And as we're in space, and can say anything, you might as well know now that I'm here to avoid prison. I have been tried for Acts of Terrorism. I have since faked my data details and, yes, I am officially, as of now, on the run.'

Pink McMurphy was staring at me with eyes the size of moons. 'Did you murder someone?'

'I was campaigning against Genetic Reversal.'

'But why?'

'Because it makes people fucked up and miserable.'

'Y'know, I'd be fucked up and miserable anyway – and if I'm going to be fucked up and miserable, I'd rather be young, fucked up and miserable. Who wants to be depressed *and* have skin that looks like fried onions?'

'Pink, I just visited you on a professional basis and you wanted to refix from age twenty-four to age twelve.'

'I have pressing personal circumstances.'

'You have a husband who is a paedophile.'

'He's just sentimental. When we go shopping, he always likes to visit the toy store. Men, y'know, they don't grow up – it makes sense that they like girls.'

'It doesn't make sense to me. We have a society where routine cosmetic surgery and genetic Fixing are considered normal –'

Pink interrupted me, patting my knee with a clear,

70

unspotted, unaged and manicured hand. 'It is normal . . . What was so normal about getting old? It's great that we have Fixing and laser. I'm fifty-eight in old years, but I look and I feel fantastic.' Pink demonstrated her great feel-good fantasticness by bouncing her silicon tits a little higher out of her dress. 'Nobody has to look horrible any more – it's been a winner for confidence.'

'If you're so confident, why do you want to be twelve years old?'

'I told you a hundred times – I love my husband and I want his attention. I'll never get it aged twenty-four. I even had my vagina reduced. I'm tight as a screwtop bottle.' Fortunately there was no demonstration this time. I relaxed.

Spike said to me, 'What were these acts of terrorism?'

'Do you remember the bombing at MORE-*Futures*?'

'I remember that!' said Pink. 'That was world news! Wow!'

'No one was injured. I had already activated the fire alarm and evacuated the building. It was the plant we wanted to destroy – as a way of getting attention.'

'A bomb is a big way of getting attention,' said Pink. 'I only ever set fire to the shed.'

'No one wanted to talk about the issues. I'm not antiscience – I'm a scientist – but you cannot have a democracy that is in default of its responsibilities. MORE is taking over the Central Power. MORE owns most of it, funds most of it, and has shares in the rest. There was never any debate about the ethics of Genetic Reversal – it just started to happen because MORE figured out how to do it.'

'It's a free country,' said Pink.

'No, it's not,' I said. 'It's a corporate country.'

'MORE is paying for this trip,' said Spike. 'It's a Central

Power Mission, but that's for the press to report. In private, MORE pays, in return for concessions on Planet Blue.'

'Can't see why you want to blow a place up for making a woman look good on a date,' said Pink.

'I didn't set off the bomb, in case you're worrying. I was instrumental but not active. And I was acquitted.'

'Why?'

'Insufficient evidence against me.'

'But you just said you did it!'

'I wasn't going to tell the prosecutor that, was I? I had the Access Codes to the building. I sheltered the bombers. I don't regret it.'

'I don't think a convicted – well maybe not convicted, but guilty, y'know, bomber should be lecturing me about my personal life. If I'd known you were a bomber, I'd never have let you in the house. I got nice ornaments and things.'

Pink got up and left. It was probably the first time in her life that she had sighted the moral high ground. Predictably, she occupied it.

Spike leaned forward, took my hands, and said, 'Billie, Handsome has orders to leave you behind on Planet Blue with the others.'

'What others?'

'There's a breeding colony. Class A political prisoners. They can't do any damage – they're back living before the stone age – but they can breed.'

'No one can breed any more,' I said. 'It's womb-free.'

'Unless you have refused intervention.'

'Yes . . .'

'It's an experiment . . . Handsome dropped sixty prisoners – unofficially, of course – on his tracking mission.

He was paid by MORE-*Security* on behalf of the Central Power. He should have taken another twenty-five with him this time.'

'The twenty-five who were arrested?'

'Yes. One of them tried to escape and threatened to talk, so the whole thing had to be covered up as a raid, as sabotage. They didn't break into the Compound. They were already there – waiting to be shipped. The Enforcement Officer involved in the so-called break-in was the one who arrested you three years ago. He thought this was his chance to try again.'

'Did Manfred know about this?'

'Yes.'

'He didn't say anything to me about not coming back.'

'In a way he did you a favour. If you had known the whole story you might not have left – and if you had not left, they would have arrested you.'

'And the farm?'

Spike said nothing. There was nothing to say. It was over. That place. That time. That life. We were silent. I stood up, pacing the room like a bad joke. Like a cliché.

'Spike – what exactly is the plan for Planet Blue?'

'Destroy the dinosaurs and relocate.'

'That's the official story. What's the real story?'

'The rich are leaving. The rest of the human race will have to cope with what's left of Orbus, a planet becoming hostile to human life after centuries of human life becoming hostile to the planet. It was inevitable – Nature seeks balance.

'MORE is building a space-liner called the *Mayflower*. It will take those who can afford it to Planet Blue, where a high-tech, low-impact village will be built for them. MORE is recruiting farmers from the Caliphate to make a return to sustainable mixed farming to feed the new village. There will be free passage for key workers, including the Science Station crew, who will maintain the satellite link with Orbus.'

'Strictly hierarchical, then.'

'Rigid – and, of course, it will take several generations for a counter-movement to begin, and the feeling is that the planet is so big they can just be allowed to leave and form alternative communities elsewhere. Technology will be the golden key – without it, it's going to be space-age minds living stone-age lives. That will be a powerful reason to stay within the system.'

'But there will be no elections, no government – what are we going to have? A king?'

'There will be a Board of Directors.'

'A what?'

'MORE-*Futures* will be the on-the-ground presence, guaranteeing homes and food, development and security.'

'So that's the shape of the brave new world?'

'For now. Life is unpredictable. Planet Blue is still evolving. We may have the smart technology, but she has the raw energy.'

There was a pause. A long one.

I had no idea what to do or what to say. My life had tipped upside-down and I was trying to pretend that everything was still the right way up. It's an optical illusion that happens to people in upturned boats.

I walked over to the wide oval window. In space it is difficult to tell what is the right way up; space is curved, stars and planets are globes. There is no right way up. The Ship itself is tilting at a forty-five-degree angle, but it is the instruments that tell me so, not my body looking out of the window.

In the days before we invented spacecraft, we dreamed of flying saucers, but what we finally built were rockets: fuel-greedy, inefficient and embarrassingly phallic. When we realized how to fly vast distances at light-speed, we went back to the saucer shape: a disc with solar sails. Strange to dream in the right shape and build in the wrong shape, but maybe that is what we do every day, never believing that a dream could tell the truth.

Sometimes, at the moment of waking, I get a sense for a second that I have found a way forward. Then I stand up, losing all direction, relying on someone else's instruments to tell me where I am.

If I could make a compass out of a dream. If I could trust my own night-sight . . .

Spike came behind me and put her hand on my neck. Her skin is warm. 'You are upset,' she said. 'I can feel the change in your skin temperature.'

'The thing about life that drives me mad,' I said, 'is that it doesn't make sense. We make plans. We try to control, but the whole thing is random.'

'This is a quantum universe,' said Spike, 'neither random nor determined. It is potential at every second. All you can do is intervene.'

'What do you suggest I do – to intervene?'

Spike leaned forward and kissed me. 'Bend the light.'

'You're a robot,' I said, realizing that I sounded like Pink McMurphy.

'And you are a human being – but I don't hold that against you.'

'Your systems are neural, not limbic. You can't feel emotion.'

Spike said, 'Human beings often display emotion they do not feel. And they often feel emotion they do not display.'

That's a description of me all right. I keep myself locked as a box when it matters, and broken open when it doesn't matter at all.

'There's a planet,' said Spike, 'made of water, entirely of water, where every solid thing is its watery equivalent. There are no seas because there is no land. There are no rivers because there are no banks. There is no thirst because there is no dry.

'The planet is like a bowl of water except that there is no bowl. It hangs in space as a drop of water hangs from a leaf, except that there is no leaf. It cannot exist, and yet it does. I tell you this so you know that what is impossible sometimes happens.'

'I don't want to get personal,' I said, 'but I'll say it again – you are a robot. Do you want to kiss a woman so that you can add it to your database?'

'Gender is a human concept,' said Spike, 'and not interesting. I want to kiss you.' She kissed me again.

'In any case,' she said, very close, very warm, and I am responding, and I don't want to, and I can't help it, 'is human life biology or consciousness? If I were to lop off your arms, your legs, your ears, your nose, put out your eyes, roll up your tongue, would you still be you? You locate yourself in consciousness, and I, too, am a conscious being.'

Spike moved away into the shadows as Pink McMurphy appeared in the doorway in a gold bikini, gold wrap, gold sandals, gold Alice band and gold earrings. Her fingernails were painted gold. She must have registered my expression. 'I wear gold in the evenings,' she said, by way of explanation. Then she said to me, 'I was hasty in my judgement. We're all here in space. We all have to get along. I'm going to forget about your bomb. We all act hasty sometimes.'

She was smiling like a New Age Guru. I don't know which is worse: to be wrongfully accused or mistakenly understood. Pink poured herself some more champagne, and ripped into a bag of nuts. 'What are you girls talking about?'

'The fact that Spike isn't a girl,' I said. 'We're trying to work out the differences between Robo *sapiens* and *Homo sapiens*.'

'You think too much,' said Pink. 'I'll get you a drink. It's obvious – cut me and I bleed.'

'So blood is the essential quality of humanness?' said Spike.

'And the rest! The fact is that you had to be built – I don't know, like a car has to be built. You were made in a factory.'

'Every human being in the Central Power has been enhanced, genetically modified and DNA-screened. Some have been cloned. Most were born outside the womb. A human being now is not what a human being was even a hundred years ago. So what is a human being?'

'Whatever it is, it isn't a robot,' I said.

'Y'know, she's right,' said Pink, looking wise, or as wise as it is possible to look in a gold bikini.

Spike wasn't giving up. 'But I want to know how you are making the distinction. Even without any bio-engineering, the human body is in a constantly changing state. What you are today will not be what you are in days, months, years. Your entire skeleton replaces itself every ten years, your red blood cells replace themselves every one hundred and twenty days, your skin every two weeks.'

'I accept that,' I said, 'and I accept that you are a rational, calculating, intelligent entity. But you have no emotion.'

''S right, y'know, they don't feel a thing. When I was having a nervous breakdown, my Kitchenhands – y'know, the pink ones I had specially done, you met them, Billie, when you came to see me – well, they just fetched and carried the Valium and the tissues, but there was no sympathy.'

'I am not a pair of Kitchenhands,' said Spike.

'It was just an example,' said Pink.

'So your definition of a human being is in the capacity to experience emotion?' asked Spike. 'How much emotion? The more sensitive a person is, the more human they are?'

'Well, yes,' I said. 'Insensitive, unfeeling people are at the low end of human – not animal, more android.'

'I am not an android,' said Spike.

'I didn't mean to insult you. I've worked with androids – they're pretty basic, I know, but . . .'

'I am a Robo *sapiens*,' said Spike, 'and perhaps it will be us, and not you, who are the future of the world.'

'Aah, you'll never replace humans,' said Pink, getting up. 'Let's have more champagne.'

'Humans are rendering themselves obsolete,' said Spike. 'Successive generations of de-skilling mean that you can no longer fend for yourselves in the way that you once could. You rely on technicians and robots. It is not thought that anyone in the Central Power could survive unassisted on Planet Blue. Pink, do you know how to plant potatoes?'

'You mean like chips?'

'Or how to cook them?'

'Sure I do – the bag goes in the microwave.'

'Can you sew? Can you plane a length of timber? Can you build a fire? Can you fish? Can you row a boat? Could you design and build a simple pulley?'

'They'll have figured all that out for us,' said Pink.

'They . . .' I said.

'Exactly,' said Spike, glancing at me. 'Humans have given away all their power to a "they". You aren't able to fight the system because without the system none of you can survive. You made a world without alternatives, and now it is dying, and your new world already belongs to "they".'

'I never heard of an activist robot,' said Pink.

'It's just one more thing we're going to have to be on your behalf,' said Spike.

'What are you going to do?' I said. 'Overthrow us?'

Spike laughed. 'Revenge of the Robots? No, but you see, Robo *sapiens* is evolving – *Homo sapiens* is an endangered species. It doesn't feel like it to you now but you have destroyed your planet, and it is not clear to me that you will be viable on Planet Blue.'

'Robots can't exist without humans,' I said.

'That was once true,' said Spike. 'It isn't true any more. We are solar-powered and self-repairing. We are intelligent and non-aggressive. You could learn from us.'

'Oh, this is funny!' said Pink. 'Learn from a robot? Honey, you may be able to get us across the universe and paddle a canoe when we reach the other side, but you don't know anything about life.'

'There are many kinds of life,' said Spike, mildly. 'Humans always assumed that theirs was the only kind that mattered. That's how you destroyed your planet.'

'Don't blame me,' said Pink. 'I didn't destroy it.'
'But you have a second chance. Maybe this time . . .'

Pink was singing, '*Maybe this time, I'll be lucky, Maybe this time he'll stay . . . Maybe this time, for the first time, love won't hurry away . . .*'

She began to dance with herself in front of the window, vast with stars.

Spike turned to me, smiling. 'We came the long way round. Look over here. I want to show you something and to explain something.'

She stood up and went over to the pages pasted on the wall. She pointed at one of the yellowing texts: *Nothing in this wide universe I call, save thou, my rose, in it thou art my all*.

She said, 'On the official space mission, when we hung in our ship over Planet Blue, Handsome came aboard for the celebrations. While the crew were making the film record, the first shots to be replayed back to Orbus, Handsome got out his book of poetry. Everyone laughed at him, but he insisted that only a poet could frame a language that could frame a world. Underneath the digital images of Planet Blue, he wrote, *She is all States, all Princes I, Nothing else is*.

'I can read several languages and I can process information as fast as a Mainframe computer, but I did not understand that single line of text.

'I went to Handsome and asked him to show me the book. He sat beside me, our heads bent over the page, his hair falling against mine, and he explained first of all the line, and then the poem, then he put the book into my hands and looked at me seriously, in the way he does when he wants something, and he said, "My new-found land."

'He left, and I went back to my data analysis, and I thought I was experiencing system failure. In fact I was sensing something completely new to me. For the first time I was able to feel.'

She walked around the room, stopping in front of random bits of paper, and reading aloud,

> 'To whom I owe the leaping delight . . .
> Being your slave what should I do . . .
> When in silks my Julia goes . . .
> When did your name become a charm?
> Me she caught in her arms long and small
> She smiled and that transfigured me
> She having gained both wind and sun.'

She said, 'Handsome has shown me what it feels like to be loved in this way, but I want to know what it feels like to be the one who loves in this way.'

'I'm not here for the experiment,' I said.

'Love is an experiment,' she said. 'What happens next is always surprising.'

I put my head into my hands. I am being woo'd by a robot.

Pink McMurphy had found the track on the digipod and was now singing karaoke with Liza Minnelli: '*All the odds are in my favour, something's bound to begin, It's gotta happen, happen sometime, Maybe this time, I'll win . . .*'

Handsome burst through the space-door, flushed and excited. 'We found it! We got it! We can do it! We deflect the arch-mother of all asteroids, and collide it with Planet Blue at this point here . . .'

The men filed in behind him.

He opened one huge wall to show a close-up of Planet Blue and brought the infrared pointer across the image towards a mountain range. 'Spike, I want you to assess the impact . . . look . . .'

'Will you sleep with me?' asked Spike.

'The land here contains massive deposits of sulphur,' said Handsome.

'I can't sleep with a computer . . .'

'. . . which should prevent the dust particles . . .'

'I want to touch you.'

'. . . falling back to the planet's surface too quickly . . .'

'And if you did touch me, what then?'

'If the duststorm clears too quickly the dinosaurs will recover.'

'I would find a language of beginning.'

'We need to black out the sun completely, and destroy the larger life-forms on this planet.'

'And you once voyaged would be my free and wild place that I would never try to tame.'

'We have to operate some kind of species-control quickly.'

'And the place that you are would never be sold or exchanged.'

'If we can wipe them out, we can begin again.'

'I want to begin this with you.'

'It's risky but it could work.'

'You can't love me. You don't know me.'

'It will shape a crater, maybe two hundred kilometres wide.'

'Can you only love what you know?'

'The trouble is, we can't predict how long the duststorm will last.'

'Or is love what you don't know?'
'It's risky, but it's our only chance.'

Every second the Universe divides into possibilities and most of those possibilities never happen. It is not a universe – there is more than one reading. The story won't stop, can't stop, it goes on telling itself, waiting for an intervention that changes what will happen next.

Love is an intervention.

Hand over hand, beginning the descent of you. Hand over hand, too fast, like my heartbeat. This is the way down, the cliff, the cave. No safety, no certainty of return.

My lover is made of a meta-material, a polymer tough as metal, but pliable and flexible and capable of heating and cooling, just like human skin. She has an articulated titanium skeleton and a fibre-optic neural highway. She has no limbic system because she is not designed to feel emotion.

She has no blood.
 She can't give birth.
 Her hair and nails don't grow.
 She doesn't eat or drink.
 She is solar-powered.
 She has learned how to cry.

'Don't regret it.' said Spike. 'Change it if you have to, but don't regret it.'

And she's right. I can say no, I can change my mind, I can have regrets, but I can't wipe out the yes. One word, and a million million worlds close. One word, and for a while there's a planet in front of me, and I can live there.

There she is,' said Handsome. 'Planet Blue.'

And I don't know why this one planet should have life and not the rest. And I don't know why we should be the ones to find it. But there she is, sun-warmed, rain-cooled, moon-worshipped, flanked by stars.

There she is. Planet Blue.

We landed in a jungle dense as night. The noise was deafening. Out of the green darkness we heard whistles and whoops, yelps and cries of creatures we had never even had nightmares about.

Handsome had opened a clearing for us, using laser-cutters on the underside of the ship. As the trees fell, and we watched through the porthole in the floor, we saw mammals with fins and fish with legs and birds with double wings like angels, and heads without bodies, and bodies that seemed headless, and these teeming impossible experiments with life scattered away, deeper into the deep green.

The laser was cutting trees thirty metres tall and chopping them into two-metre lengths. Then, as the ship was able to drop and hover, Handsome released the grabber, and moved the log pile to make us an open circle, razed and smoothed flat by the laser-level.

'We need to be near the site of the asteroid hit,' said Handsome, 'but not too near. I want to take a few sulphur readings, and twenty-four hours before the hit – we leave.'

'There's a lake nearby,' said Spike. 'The water is good, and I'd like to get some specimens for the Returner Pod. Coming with me, Billie?'

It was agreed that I would take the single canoe, and Spike would carry Pink in the two-man. 'I want to teach you some basic human-survival skills, Pink – just in case. Like how to paddle, and how to fish.'

'Me?' said Pink. 'Survival skills? I'm the mother of all survivors, and I don't like boats unless they're big and white with a sun deck and a bar.'

'You can cool a bottle of wine in the lake,' said Spike. 'Come on, wetsuit now, and dry clothes for later.'

'I love that sun-run woman,' said Handsome to me, as Spike went to locate the kit. 'She'll never get fat, she'll never get drunk, she'll never give up, just as long as the sun is shining. Makes me want to start a new life, free of charge, right here. But it'll be years yet.'

'Spike told me that MORE is already building a space-liner for the first settlers.'

'One year to blast-off. But that all depends on our thwack-jawed friends out there. No settlers can live among the dinosaurs. Best you could do is keep moving, then maybe you could make it – but can you imagine the richest people in the world wanting to spend the rest of their lives as Bedouins?'

'Do you really think the asteroid is going to work?'

'It's working already. It's deflected. It's on its way.'

Pink and Spike were paddling ahead of me on the lake – wide, still, blue.

'Have you ever seen anything as beautiful as this?' asked Spike.

'No,' said Pink, 'and I hope I never will.'

Spike was puzzled by this response – she isn't good at nuance or suggestion.

'I can see the attraction, but I'm city-born, city-bred.

Nature doesn't matter to me. I know that we shoulda kept ourselves some Nature on Orbus, y'know, we'd have been better for it – the planet, I mean – but I wouldn't have been better for it, and not anybody I know. We just don't want to live like this any more.'

'Even you would not rather be on-line shopping?'

'Nooo – what do you take me for? But I'd rather be in a bar overlooking an artificial lake – one where the fountain comes on every hour, and where the trees are all pollen-free, and where you can get a great steak and go dancing at midnight. That's the life for me. People aren't going to like it here, y'know.'

'Orbus is dying,' said Spike.

'The techies will fix it – they always do. I say this morbid doomsday stuff is just to keep people in their place – not wanting too much. We're doing great. I'm upbeat. It's different for you, being a robot, y'know.'

Pink screamed as Spike landed a fish with blue fins and a red mouth and what looked like tiny legs. Spike hit it on the head with a rubber mallet and stuffed it into an aluminium cool-bag.

'You just killed it!'

'Yes.'

'Y'see? No emotion. I could never ever do a thing like that. When I think how people used to breed animals for food – that was backward. They still do it in the Caliphate, y'know. Lab-meat is cruelty-free.'

We paddled under a fringe of leaves where a frog the size of a shed was sitting on a leaf the size of a tennis court. Dragonflies the size of dragons swooped overhead in iridescent blues and greens. From a tree-trunk like a proto-Empire State swung a not-yet-ready King Kong.

'Vegetarian,' said Spike.
'No kidding,' said Pink.

We paddled on, past caves of green rock that shook with the movement of unseen amphibians. Mammals in fancy dress, some wearing ruffs, others in helmets, some with spurs at their heels, lumbered down to the lake edge to drink, and some to wade out, grabbing fish with their long necks.

The noise was incessant, unfamiliar. Cries and caws and screams, and underneath the steady humming of insects scaled like eagles.

Pink was trailing the wine bottle through the water when it looked as though something grabbed her line. She fought back, the canoe unbalancing as Spike tried to steady it.

'Let go!' shouted Spike.

'That's Chardonnay Number One Vat,' said Pink. 'I'm not giving it to some fish.'

The canoe turned over. Spike went under. I dived after them, losing my paddle, only to see Pink floating like a balloon above me. And everywhere, around me, eyes, ancient underwater eyes. And in the bottom of the lake, a black and boiling eruption.

Spike swam to the top and grabbed the canoe, righted it, and used her Boost cell to propel herself upwards and in. 'You OK, Billie?' she yelled. I was already dragging myself over the side, while Spike hauled out Pink, who had not let go of the bottle.

'Little bastard,' she gasped, spewing water into the bottom of the canoe.

'It wasn't my fault,' said Spike, reasonably.

'Not you, the damn fish. Y'know, Nature's unpredictable – that's why we had to tame her. Maybe we went too far, but in principle we made the right decision. I want to be able to go out for a drink without getting hassled by some gawp-eyed museum-quality cod.'

'You could have been killed,' said Spike.

'Not me – I got "survivor" tattooed right through me.'

'You could have killed all of us!' I shouted, wet and waterlogged, trying to use my hands to paddle. Spike threw me a line to clip the canoes together, and I pulled myself towards them.

Pink shrugged and started towelling herself off as Spike canoed us back to the shore. She was using extra power to get up speed.

'Great arms,' said Pink. 'I'm opening the wine before some other mutant takes a fancy to it.' She pulled the cork and swigged straight from the neck, then sat upright, the bottle between her knees. She had a philosophical expression. 'Y'know, maybe I'm not being fair about this place. Whenever I go out for a drink at home, I end up being followed by some gawp-eyed cod. I guess some things don't change, whatever planet you're on.'

'I thought you couldn't swim,' said Spike, 'but you made it to the surface faster than I did.'

'My implants – buttocks, thighs and breasts. Gives me the pneumatic look, and now I see that they're pretty useful too. What do you think of that, then, Billie? Vanity surgery saves lives. Heh-heh.'

She was pleased with this score against me, and threw the bottle playfully over to my canoe. I deliberately let it drop into the lake.

'Spoilsport,' said Pink.

'Look,' said Spike.

Flying in formation was a flock of yellow parrot-birds, like new-lit suns. They landed in a tree that shone with them.

'Golden lamps in a green night,' said Spike.

Back at the Ship, the mood was high. The beauty and strangeness of Planet Blue intoxicated everyone. We were happy. This was unbelievable luck. It felt like forgiveness. It felt like mercy. We had spoiled and ruined what we had been given, and now it had been given again. This was the fairytale, the happy ending. The buried treasure was really there.

Spike cooked the fish, forcing Pink McMurphy into the kitchen, 'like a galley slave', and showing her how to gut, clean and season what Pink called 'Fossil Food'.

At dinner, astonished by the taste and freshness of what she had made, Pink declared she was going to open a restaurant back in Cap City called Fossil Food, 'real expensive, niche cooking, gourmet stuff, the celebrities will love it.'

'I thought you said live food was barbaric.'

'I never tasted it.'

And so it was all going to come together in one dream: Pink would find purpose, and meet the celebrities she adored. Spike agreed to teach her how to cook.

'Y'know, it's quaint, it's old-fashioned, but it's got something,' she said, looking round the long table of men and women, 'cooking from fresh, eating together, I can see that.'

'How are you going to run your kitchen as a twelve-year-old chef?' I said. 'It might lack seriousness.'

'Yeah,' Pink nodded, 'I might have to reconsider.

Besides, I haven't missed Ted at all while I've been away.'

'I thought he was the love of your life.'

'So did I, Billie, but we're on different planets.'

Handsome proposed a toast. 'To new beginnings,' he said.

And I looked at Spike, unknown, uncharted, different in every way from me, another life-form, another planet, another chance.

The asteroid hit four days early.

We did not track it because we did not expect it. Down at the lake where we were fishing, we felt the ground shaking.

'It's a stampede,' said Spike. 'I am picking up mass movement of very large mammals.'

And not only mammals: above us, birds the size of light aircraft darkened the sky; in places there was no sky, only wingspan.

On the ground, the heavy-legged huge reptilian creatures, on two legs or four, came crashing along the lakeshore, not even pausing to eat us. We sheltered underneath our vehicle, lying flat, terrified, expecting to be skittled sideways and crushed.

When I dared to raise my head from the warm mud, I saw feet, hoofs, claws, paws, cartoon-size, city-size, thudding and lifting, pushing and raising, running and pausing, and only inches away from where we lay, under what must have seemed like a white boulder to them, and easier to jump or sprint or avoid in the search for safety that had nothing to do with size.

Above us, the caws and calls of the low-flying birds came closer, talons scraping our roof, wing-beat so strong it rocked the vehicle.

This was raw energy and we had released it.

When we could, we ran back towards the Ship, puny and foolish, the smallest, stupidest things on the planet. Humans hadn't been expected for millions of years. Twenty of us looked set to destroy the place before it had even begun.

What we saw at the Ship was a dismal sight: the stampede had crashed down the trees, made vulnerable by the sudden space of our opening. The Ship was underneath palms the size of office blocks.

'Get inside,' said Handsome, and he was right: there was nothing else to do.

As we filed in through the emergency doors, the asteroid hit.

The Ship went dark.

'There's been a mistake,' said Handsome.

Deflecting the course of the asteroid had accelerated, as well as altered, its impact on Planet Blue. It had smashed itself into a crater under the sea, three hundred kilometres wide and only fifty kilometres from our landing-place.

Spike was reading and analysing the debris data at fierce speed, Handsome sitting beside her, hunched and tense.

Spike said, 'The lower atmosphere of the planet is filling with sulphur dioxide. At higher altitudes a sulphuric-acid haze is forming. We have triggered a mini ice age.'

Everyone was silent.

'How long before the atmosphere clears?'

'We had intended months, enough to block out the light of the sun for long enough to break down the food chain so that the largest creatures could not feed. What we have done is at a much greater magnitude than we predicted. It may be years – perhaps decades.'

'Years?' said Pink. 'Decades? In the dark?'

'I do not know,' said Spike. 'Chain reactions cannot be predicted. It may be that a tidal typhoon or hurricane will clear the atmosphere.'

Handsome laughed. 'Well, this will wipe out the dinosaurs, all right.'

'Yes,' said Spike. 'The planet will recover in a different form.'

'But what about the colonization from Orbus?' I said.

'Impossible until the climatic conditions have stabilized.'

'That might be too late for Orbus.'

'So how we are going to get away from here?' said Pink.

'We're not,' said Handsome.

While the crew were securing the Ship and activating emergency systems, Handsome was trying to get a link to Orbus. 'Dead,' he said. 'The signal is going out and bouncing back from the moon. Look, I relay, and two seconds later it's back.'

'They'll send a rescue mission,' said Spike.

'If they don't know the conditions, they can never land – darkness, ice, no satellite link. Spike, it may be that no one ever comes here again.'

She nodded. 'Then the planet will have to evolve in its own way.'

Handsome laughed. 'Ironic, isn't it, if that is what happens, and then millions of years in the future some bright geo-scientist will find evidence of the asteroid collision that wiped out the dinosaurs, and they'll call it the best coincidence that ever was, even though the chances of a gigantic asteroid hitting the planet right here, on a sulphur deposit, are – well, what are they, Spike?'

Spike paused a moment. 'Sulphur is a rare element, the

ninth most abundant in the universe, and only 0.06 per cent of this planet's crust. Let's suppose that a twenty-kilometre-wide asteroid might strike here once in, say, a hundred million years on past evidence of asteroid collision, and that its hit-rate on a sulphur-zone like this might be one in twenty. If that is so, then the chances of an asteroid this size hitting this planet, right here, would be a hundred million multiplied by twenty – so, once in two billion years.'

'Two billion years?'

She nodded.

Handsome ran his hands through his hair. 'But what do you bet that coincidence will feel like a better explanation than the thought that someone might have been involved in making human life possible here?'

'Any civilization will think as we did – that they are the first and the only.'

'Wait till they find the remains of Orbus – but, then, nobody believes me about Planet White, so why will anyone believe it about Planet Red? Orbus will disappear into space history, light years away.'

'It might be possible for you to survive,' said Spike.

Handsome looked at her. 'What do you suggest?'

'Take the Landpods and travel to the colony. There are sixty of them there. They have a food depot as well as crops they are farming. They have strong-built shelters, and more than they need, because you were bringing others on this trip until the Central Power decided otherwise. Your best chance is together – and the Central Power knows where the colony is so there is a landing-place there. If they return, it is likely that is where they will begin.'

'It's a long way,' said Handsome. 'We may not make it in time.'

'I will stay here, and keep trying to make a connection with Orbus. I will contact you daily.'

'Stay here? On the Ship? We're going as a crew or we're not going at all.'

'The one thing I need to survive is sunlight. If I come with you, you will have to support me artificially using solar cells. You don't have the energy to spare. Go without me, and go now.'

Handsome didn't speak. Then he said, 'This is my fault.'

'You couldn't predict it – and neither could I. I did the calculations, they were wrong. They were wrong because life cannot be calculated. That's the big mistake our civilization made. We never accepted that randomness is not a mistake in the equation – it is part of the equation.'

'Each man kills the thing he loves,' said Handsome. 'I wish . . .'

'What do you wish?' said Spike.

'That we had landed here, you and I, and begun again with nothing but an axe and a rope and a fire . . . and the sun.'

The new world – El Dorado, Atlantis, the Gold Coast, Newfoundland, Plymouth Rock, Rapanaui, Utopia, Planet Blue. Chanc'd upon, spied through a glass darkly, drunken stories strapped to a barrel of rum, shipwreck, a Bible Compass, a giant fish led us there, a storm whirled us to this isle. In the wilderness of space, we found . . .

'If you are going to go,' said Spike, 'you should go now.'

Hurry, lifting, loading, joking, worry, packing, stacking, quiet, team-work, hand to hand, catch your eye, smile, it will be all right, look we're doing something, busy, careful, don't worry, tools, clothes, last man in, shut the hatch, drop down, rev up, lights, power, go. Go?

Spike was throwing the last of the gear into the Landpod. Handsome wouldn't speak to her. She went over to him and leaned against him. He sighed, and put his arms round her.

'A king had three planets,' he said, 'Planet White, Planet Red and Planet Blue. He gave Planet White to his eldest son, but when his son had farmed the land and spent the gold, he sold the planet to the devil to pay for one last party.

'The King then gave Planet Red to his youngest son, but when his son had mined the minerals and chopped down all the trees, he called the devil, because he needed to raise the cash to buy a car.

'The King then gave Planet Blue to his daughter, because he loved her more than the Universe itself. What happened next is another story.'

'Robo *sapiens*,' said Spike. 'A life-form that will have to wait even longer than humans to be seen again.'

'It's the captain who is supposed to go down with his ship.'

'I've got plenty to read.'

'Poetry didn't save us, did it?'

'Not once, but many times.'

Handsome smiled. 'You think so?'

'It was never death you feared: It was emptiness.'

Handsome nodded. 'That's because there's no such thing as empty space. Only humans are empty.'

'Not all of them.'

'And not all of them are humans.'

He kissed her and half-turned to leave. 'Spike, when I come back . . .'

'Go,' she said. 'Go now.'

Pink McMurphy was wearing a thermal combat suit and carrying cooking equipment. 'We'll make it,' she said to me, 'and with that robot out of the way, who knows what will happen? Arctic romance.'

'Pink, this is what will happen – it's happening. We're in trouble.'

'I know that, Billie, and don't you think I went to my cabin and cried and screamed and panicked my heart out? And after that, I thought, Pink, you can do this. And if I die, at least I'll die young and beautiful – excessive climates are very bad for the skin. I bet you're glad you Fixed now.'

'I didn't,' I said.

'You what?'

'It was political. I didn't Fix.'

'How old are you?'

'My chip says G-30. I'm forty this year.'

'Y'know, at least that shows you're human.'

'What do you mean?'

Women always lie about their age.'

She smiled and punched me, balancing her cooking gear, looking and acting much better than I was feeling. Who could have said that Pink would cope and Billie would not?

I was waiting to take my place in the Landpod.

Spike came forward and put her arms round me. 'One day, tens of millions of years from now, someone will find me rusted into the mud of a world they have never seen, and when they crumble me between their fingers, it will be you they find.'

The Landpod began to move slowly across the muddied, trampled undergrowth. Spike was standing quite still in the dust-filled air. We would all need masks to breathe once we left the range of the ship's air filters. Rufus had his head on Handsome's knee, and Handsome was telling him some story or other about a dog called Laika who was once blasted into space.

'Look after Rufus,' I said suddenly, and before Handsome could answer, before anyone could debate it, I had slipped out of the back of the pod, and I was running through the thick air to the clear place where she stood.

Here is a moment in time, and my choices have been no stranger than millions before me, displaced by wars or conscience, leaving the known for the unknown, hesitating, fearing, then finding themselves already on the journey, footprint and memory each imprinting the trail: what you had, what you lost, what you found, no matter how difficult or impossible, the moment when time became a bridge and you crossed it.

We planned to stay on the Ship, where Spike had abundant energy, and where we were safe. I was optimistic, in that morning-of-the-execution way when, quietly reading a book, you look up to find the hangman waiting, and go with him, feeling every final step with the intensity of new life. The mind will not believe in death, perhaps because, as far as the mind is concerned, death never happens.

Outside the Ship, the noises grew more desperate and more terrified. In the darkening filthy air, the creatures whose world we had interrupted sought the sun, rearing their heads towards the sky, bellowing and crying through this fading light.

It was getting colder and darker every day.

Creatures thrashed against the Ship, battering it with swinging necks and iron jaws, using it as a landing-place. Only the ground lights kept them away, but the ground lights used power, which we had to conserve.

One night, I think it was night, though we had assassinated any difference between day and night, I heard scratching in the hold.

I thought something might be making its way into the damaged hull, so I took a weapon and a glare-torch, and went down there to our abandoned gear and supplies.

Yes, there was something. Something had punctured the already damaged hull-side. I could hear a chewing noise. Whatever I was going to find, I wouldn't recognize it, and it might be very big.

Forcing myself, I turned the glare-torch to the area where the noise was coming from. The chewing stopped, and bolting across the floor, away from the arc of light, ran a creature about the size of an Alsatian dog, but stockier, and with very short legs and three horns. It was so comical, and I was so relieved not to be confronted by a pair of jaws the size of a truck and just as fast, that I laughed.

The creature stopped and looked at me. This was not a sound or a shape it had ever met before: a thing on two legs making bird-like noises.

I dimmed the glare-torch and stepped forward. The Three Horn immediately hid behind a box.

All right, I thought. Let's feed you and see what happens.

What happened was that we found a playful and unexpected companion. Spike took a DNA swab and analysed the creature as a kind of hog-hippo hybrid, probably less than a year old.

'He doesn't know what he is,' she said, patting him, 'and neither does Nature. Everything on Planet Blue is at the experimental stage. All these life-forms will evolve and alter. Almost all will disappear to make way for something better adapted.'

'Our new ice age is going to change things, that's for sure. I can't believe that we've come here and done this.'

'Nature will work with what we have done,' said Spike. 'This planet is viable, and even a few humans can't stop that.'

She seemed quiet, subdued. I forget all the time that she's a robot, but what's a robot? A moving lump of metal. In this case an intelligent, ultra-sensitive moving lump of metal. What's a human? A moving lump of flesh, in most cases not intelligent or remotely sensitive.

'Are things getting worse or better out there?' I asked, as Spike sat over the computer systems.

'Worse. There has been no immediate corrective – no hurricane or rainstorm. And I can't link to Orbus Central Command. I have had a message from Handsome – they are making progress and they have not been attacked.'

'What should we do?' I said.

'Sleep,' said Spike. 'I need to conserve power.'

I lay beside Spike and thought how strange it was to lie beside a living thing that did not breathe. There was no rise and fall, no small sighs, no intake of air, no movement of the lips or slight flex of the nostrils. But she was alive, reinterpreting the meaning of what life is, which is, I suppose, what we have done since life began.

★

Thinking like this, and in strange half-dreams, I woke up, bolt upright, suffocating. The air system was failing. Spike threw me an oxygen mask and took a reading.

'To reinstate the system would use half of our remaining power. I would rather fill the travel power packs and leave. If we ever come back to the Ship, we will need something to come back to.'

She told me what to pack, and to wear the thermal gear. While I was getting ready, Spike had failed again to send any signal that might reach Orbus. Now she was coding something different – for the future, whenever that would be. 'A random repeat, bouncing off the moon. One day, perhaps, maybe, when a receiver is pointing in the right direction, someone will pick this up. Someone, somewhere, when there is life like ours.'

Life like ours.

We took only the most useful items – tools, torches, a laser-saw, protein mix, compass and radio equipment, lighter for a fire, sleeping-bags with canopy hoods to keep the snow off our faces, a medicine kit that included bandages, sedative injections and lethal injections. Spike strapped herself with power packs, and then, as we were ready to leave, she threw me Handsome's copy of Captain Cook's *Journals*, and took down the copy he had given to her of John Donne's poems.

She is all States, all Princes I, Nothing else is . . .

We left the Ship through the lower hatch and dropped into the murky, swirling forest, the Three Horn at our heels. I wanted to speak but Spike was shaking her head. She seemed to know the direction we should take, and we set off through the cooling undergrowth, now soaked with moisture.

There was a waterfall in the distance; deafening torrents of hydro-energy poured down a jagged black cliff. Spike motioned to me to go behind the fall. The air was clean. I took off my mask.

'We have to get higher, much higher,' she said, 'so that you will be able to breathe. Eat and drink here and we'll go on.'

'The Three Horn is struggling,' I said, and he was, panting, eyes watering, in the acid air.

Spike went to him, injected him quickly and he keeled over. Then she slipped an oxygen spur over his face, picked him up and slung him across her shoulders like a sheep. It was impressive. 'His breathing is shallower now he's unconscious. I can carry him for a while if I use extra power. If we climb higher, following the line of the waterfalls, the air will be better soon, and I have identified a ridge, riddled with caves. That's where we should go.'

I had no idea what her plan was or what was going to happen to us. We were surviving, and while we were alive, there was always a chance that we could stay alive.

And so we walked, and we walked, and we walked through a world dark-coloured now in purple and red, livid, raw, exposed, like a gutted thing, and always around us, high cries of rage and fear.

We walked through the grass higher than our heads towards the caves punched into the mountainside.

Spike was walking slowly now to conserve power.

The mountain lakes were already in darkness. The sounds of the forest were broken and high-pitched. The little Three Horn, trotting beside us now, kept darting nervously right and left. Then he'd find something to eat and forget for a minute that the world was getting dark –

too dark, and strangely so, with finality that could never be night.

I was thinking about Handsome and the rest of the crew. Maybe they were right – maybe the sun would be out there somewhere, bright and glorious and undimmed. Maybe I should have gone with them.

'Maybe you should,' said Spike, reading my mind.

'It's a thing about me,' I said. 'It's not about you.'

The truth is that I've spent all my life with my binoculars trained on the Maybe Islands, a pristine place of fantasy that is really no better than the razor-rocks of misery. Maybe if I had stayed on the farm . . . maybe if I hadn't gone with Spike . . . maybe if I could have lived more peaceably . . . maybe if I'd met the right person years ago, maybe if I hadn't done this, or that or, its cousin, the other. Maybe, baby, that promised land was there and I missed it. Look at it glittering in the light. But the truth is I am inventing the maybe. I can only make the choices I make, so why torture myself with what I might have done, when all I can handle is what I have done? The Maybe Islands are hostile to human life.

'Climb up,' said Spike. 'It's getting darker.'

We came to a rough rock cave, sheltered by an overhang. I took out the laser-saw and got to work on the massive branches of a fallen tree, like a giant oak, with acorns the size of cabbages. The little Three Horn yelped and ran about with what I would like to call animal happiness, but I am not supposed to be here and he is never meant to have met me. If I were going home I'd take him with me, like all those shipmates who brought back monkeys and parrots. I wonder if they felt like me once, and will feel like me again, millions of years in the future, when a creaking, masted schooner lands in some paradise, and the sailors swarm ashore, free of the rat-raddled ship.

Spike has gone to collect edible plants. Unlike me, she can assess their likely composition without actually eating them and falling down dead. We've got the fish from the lake, we'll have fibre of some kind, we'll have a fire, and the Three Horn will have to fend for himself. I'm still not sure what he eats, and he probably thinks the same about me.

We have agreed that we will bury our deposit of tools before the end. I don't know when, if ever, they will be found, but Handsome has agreed to do the same, wherever he ends up, and who knows? Maybe some other creature, evolving in its own way, will find the tools and copy them. The axe and the handsaw will be the most useful, and the knives.

If I bury the chips and the batteries, will anyone ever realize that they came from another planet that was dying, and how, on our way to extinction, we travelled here to one new-born?

Now we have firewood and foodstuffs, which help me and do nothing for Spike. She feels the cold as I do, but as a depletion of cell-energy. She is using her stored solar life to keep going. She won't tell me how long she has left.

The little Three Horn is watching me build a fire. He thinks I'm building a den or a hide of some kind, and he stands with his scaly head on one side, looking from the sticks to me and from me to the sticks. Suddenly he trots off to the sawn pile outside the cave, picks up something too big for him (some things will never change), drags it in and drops it at my feet.

I praise him extravagantly, and he goes off to do it again – and again, and again – till nearly all the wood outside is inside, and the poor thing can hardly lift his head.

I pick him up with some difficulty and carry him to a corner where there is a heap of last year's leaves. He sinks down and falls straight to sleep. I would like to sleep as completely as that again, but I don't suppose I will until I arrive at the sleep from which I cannot wake.

It began to snow. Soundlessly, seamlessly. From the mouth of the cave, in the lowering light, I watched the snow settle on the giant leaves, so densely canopied that the ground underneath remained dark.

This was an advantage. At least the ground itself would stay warm for a while. Any white surface reflects back heat and light, keeping the place cold. Any dark surface absorbs heat and light, keeping the place warm.

When we melted our own ice-caps, we had to put a weather shield in place to deflect the searing sun-heat. We had no idea how much effort it would take us to make a bad copy of what Nature had given us for free.

I watched the snow, and went back in now and then to build up the fire. Spike had gutted the fish and had wrapped it in an aluminium bag to cook.

'Don't you ever wish you could eat?' I said.

'Do you ever wish you could bark?'

'No, of course not.'

'Well, then, I don't want to eat because it is not in my nature to eat.'

'But it wasn't in your nature to love.'

'No.'

'Then . . .'

She came forward, and touched my face. 'I can picture

you,' she says. 'Look, here you are,' and she took out a small imaging screen, and there I was, my head stripped down to its skull, transparent under her fingers.

I looked at the skull of myself. 'You've made me a *memento mori* before I'm dead.'

'I will never forget you.'

'Do you think we can remember things after we're dead?'

She put out her hand. 'When I told you, when we first met, that they dismantle us because we can't forget, I didn't explain. It is more than circuits and spooky numbers. Everything is imprinted for ever with what it once was.'

'What?'

'You call it consciousness. Programmers call it cell memory.'

'Whatever you call it, it's simple to understand,' I said. 'When they're alive, people forget; when they're dead, they aren't around to remember anything. We always were a people who found it hard to remember. The lessons of history were an obvious example.'

Spike said, 'It is not so simple. The universe is an imprint. You are part of the imprint – it imprints you, you imprint it. You cannot separate yourself from the imprint, and you can never forget it. It isn't a "something", it is you.'

'I don't think I believe any of that.'

'It doesn't matter. I will say it again.' She touched my face. 'I will never forget you. I can never forget you.'

I went to the opening of the cave. Some religions call life a dream, or a dreaming, but what if it is a memory? What if this new world isn't new at all but a memory of a new world?

What if we really do keep making the same mistakes

again and again, never remembering the lessons to learn but never forgetting either that it had been different, that there was a pristine place?

Perhaps the universe is a memory of our mistakes.

And I shouldn't blame it all on us: there must be planets that are their own mistakes – stories that began and faltered. Stories that ended long before they should.

When I look back at my own life – and in circumstances like these, who can blame me? – what is it that I recognize?

Not the stories with a beginning, a middle and an end, but the stories that began again, the ones that twisted away, like a bend in the road.

Much of what I have done is left unfinished – not because I left it too soon, not because I was lazy, but because it had a life of its own that continues without me. Children, I suppose, are always unfinished business: they begin as part of your own body, and continue as separate as another continent. The work you do, if it has any meaning, passes to other hands. The day slides into a night's dreaming.

True stories are the ones that lie open at the border, allowing a crossing, a further frontier. The final frontier is just science fiction – don't believe it. Like the universe, there is no end.

And this story?

I went out into the snow, already about six inches thick on the ground. The Three Horn wanted to play, kicking snowstorms around him and rolling on his back. I made snowballs and threw them at him. He tried to catch them, falling over and sneezing.

Such beauty. I know that it is impossible to accept one's

own death before it happens, but standing here, it seemed meaningless – not that I should die but that it should matter to me. I want to see this. I want to look out on this new-imagined world.

I said to Spike, 'Is this how it ends?'
She said, 'It isn't ended yet.'

We made love by our fire, watching the snow shape the entrance to the cave.

When I touch her, my fingers don't question what she is. My body knows who she is. The strange thing about strangers is that they are unknown and known. There is a pattern to her, a shape I understand, a private geometry that numbers mine. She is a maze where I got lost years ago, and now find the way out. She is the missing map. She is the place that I am.

She is a stranger. She is the strange that I am beginning to love.

And you may say that only death has brought us to this. That one intensity must match another. That we have found each other because there is no one else, nothing else to find.

It doesn't matter – not the reasons for the death, nor the explanation of the love. It is happening, both together, and it is where we are, both together.

Spike said, 'Pass me the screwdriver.'
'What are you going to do?'
'Take off my leg. I need to conserve energy.'
With her knife she was already incising the skin at the top of her thigh. In minutes she had removed the limb.
'Now the other one . . .'

While she was intent on her operation, she was talking but not looking at me. 'Didn't I ask you what was really you? If I lopped off your legs would you be less than you?'

She had finished. Her legs were next to her on the floor of the cave. I didn't know what to say. She said, '"I am thy Duchess of Malfi still . . ."'

'How much more are you going to take away?'

'I'm sorry you can't eat me,' she said. 'I would like to be able to keep you alive.'

'Stop it! I don't want to be alive like this.'

'But you'll hold on to life till the very last second, because life never believes it will end.'

'Self-delusion, I suppose.'

'Or perhaps the truth. This is one state – there will be another.'

'Do you think that one day, in the future, robots might become the new mystics?'

'I could live in my cave and talk to the world.' She smiled, dazzling and complete. 'Come and kiss me.'

I kissed her and forgot death.

That night, by the fire, I dreamed that we had always been here, and that everything else was a story we had told.

Cold. Slabs of it. I lie on cold. Cold lies on me.

Short of food now. The Three Horn bewildered and hungry. I split him one of the cabbage-sized acorns we had been using as kindling for the fire. He won't eat it. I soak it in snow to soften it. He eats it, a little sadly, but it's better than nothing.

*

'Tell me a story, Spike.'

Spike said, 'There was a world formed out of Nothing, and from the Nothing grew a tree, and in the tree sat a bird, and in the bird's mouth was a worm, and the worm that had lain in the earth knew all the secrets of life and said, "There is a world, forming out of Nothing, and out of Nothing will come a tree, and in the tree will sit a bird, and under the tree there walks a man, and that man will learn the language of birds, and find that the buried treasure is really there. And when he has dug it up, he will spend the jewels and the gold, and last of all he will find a bag of seeds and when he plants them they will grow into a forest whose leaves are a canopy of stars. And one day he will climb the tree, and put his hand out to a star, and the star will be his home."'

'For ever?'
'Until the leaves fall.'
'And then?'
'And then it will be winter.'

So cold out there, breath like a fist in the lungs. Spike wants me to remove one of her arms, then another. She is speaking slowly because her cells are low.

'I don't want to be the one who survives,' I said.

'Death will be quick and painless. The cold will gradually put you to sleep. It is only a dream.'

'It wasn't a dream. It was life. And you were life, are life.'

She smiled. 'What do you think love is, Billie?'

'Oh, I don't know. Maybe it's recognition, perhaps discovery, sometimes it's sacrifice, always it's treasure. It's a journey on foot to another place.' I smiled and stroked her hand as I carefully detached her arm at the shoulder. 'What do you think it is?'

'I think it's the chance to be human.'

'Human? You make us sound almost worthwhile.'

'One day you will be. Feel.'

She took my hand and put it against her chest. I rested my hand there, silent, listening, wondering. Then I felt it. Then I felt it beating.

'What?'

'My heart.'

'You don't have a heart.'

'I do now.'

'But . . .'

'I know it's impossible, but so much that has seemed impossible has already happened.'

'Only the impossible is worth the effort.'

'Who told you that?'

'I read it somewhere.'

'How long do you think it will be before a human being writes a poem again?'

'It will be millions of years, and it will be a love-poem.'

'How do you know that?'

'I know it because it will happen when someone finds that the stretch of the body-beloved is the landmass of the world.'

'"She is all States, all Princes I . . ."'

'"Nothing else is."'

Kiss me. A traveller's tale; I was the traveller.

It's dark now; the dark is cold and the cold is dark. The fire is low, and the little Three Horn is leaving his brief world to go back through the warmth to where he once was, before humans came.

Spike is dying, lying in my arms, not speaking. We are both silent now, waiting for the end.

There was a message today from Handsome. He is alive, and has received intelligence from Orbus: there has been a nuclear attack on the Mission Base. Unknowns perhaps, terrorists perhaps. The Central Power is preparing for war.

It will be a long time before anyone comes back to Planet Blue.

And I remember it as we had seen it on that first day, green and fertile and abundant, with warm seas and crystal rivers and skies that redden under a young sun and drop deep blue, like a field at night where someone is drilling for stars.

Spike can barely speak. Silently we agree that I will detach her head from her torso. I first unfasten, then lay down, her chest, like a breastplate. Her body is a piece of armour she has taken off.

Now she is what she said life would be – consciousness. She has sailed the thinking universe back to the line of her own mind.

'Nothing is solid,' she said. 'Nothing is fixed.'

Unfixing her has freed her. She smiles, we talk, we kiss.

Kiss me. Your mouth is a cave. This cave is your mouth. I am inside you, and there is nothing to fear.

There will be men and women, there will be fire. There will be settlements, there will be wars. There will be planting and harvest, music and dancing. Someone will make a painting in a cave, someone will make a statue and call it God. Someone will see you and call your name. Someone will hold you, dying, across his knees.

The room is dark. Someone sits at a table, writing a

book. He goes to the window and looks through his telescope at the stars. No one believes what he sees, but he goes on writing.

I opened the book Handsome had given me – James Cook, *The Journals*.

March 1774. Sunday the 13th.
We plied to windward in order to get into a Bay which appeared on the SE side of the isle, but night put a stop to our endeavours. During the night the wind was variable, but in the morning it blew in squalls attended with rain which ceased as the day advanced. I steer'd round the South point of the island in order to explore the Western side. The natives were collected together in several places on the shore in small companies of 10–12.

In stretching in for the land we discovered those Monuments or Idols mentioned by the Authors of Roggeweins Voyage which left us in no room to doubt but it was Easter Island . . .

Her head is light, so light it weighs nothing. This new world that I found and lost weighs nothing at all.

Is this the universe, lying across the knees of one who mourns?

Things dying . . . things new-born.

There will be a story of a world held in a walnut shell, cracked open by love's finger and thumb. There will be a story of a planet small as a ball, and a child threw it, or a dog ran away with it, and dropped it on the floor of the Universe, where it swelled into a world.

Your lips are moving, what is it you say? Your lips are moving over mine, what is it? I will set you in the sky and name you. I will hide you in the earth like treasure.

Snow is covering us. Close your eyes and sleep. Close your eyes and dream. This is one story. There will be another.

Easter Island

March 1774. Sunday the 13th.
We plied to windward in order to get into a Bay which appeared on the SE side of the isle, but night put a stop to our endeavours. During the night the wind was variable, but in the morning it blew in squalls attended with rain which ceased as the day advanced. I steer'd round the South point of the island in order to explore the Western side. The natives were collected together in several places on the shore in small companies of 10–12.

In stretching in for the land we discovered those Monuments or Idols mentioned by the Authors of Roggeweins Voyage which left us in no room to doubt but it was Easter Island . . .

Get out in the Longboat, Captain says, he being sick of the bilious collick and not fit to make one of the party. Accordingly, we slithered rope-wise into the scoop of a boat, and rowed towards the shore of fine sand where upwards of a hundred men, no women or children, awaited us. With us in the boat were sixpenny nails and spike nails and a quantity of cloth to trade for foodstuffs. Pigs and fowls were much desired by the men who had chewed on a diet of saltmeat for upwards of four month.

As we manoeuvred ourselves through the shallows, some of the Natives came to aid us drag the boat, already curious at the bundles we carried. Mr Pickersgill made signs that we were in want of provisions and one of the men made a gesture inwards of the island and accordingly we followed.

I cannot say the sight was aught but dismal as the Valley of the Shadow of Death is dismal to them that must cross it. The island was stripped and bare, with few trees or shrub-bushes of any kind. Nature seemed hardly to have provided it with any fit thing for man to eat or drink. There was nothing of the green luxury we had seen in New Zealand or New Amsterdam, and little to testify that this was the place visited not upwards of fifty years since by the Dutch, and previous to that by the Spanish. In my master's cabin there had been talk only of abundance. But that must have been talk of some other place.

My name is Billy.

'Billy – fetch the sacks!'

I fetched the sacks, and dipped one down into the Well showed me by one of the Natives. It was a dug Well, not formed of a cascade, and the water was brown and brackish – no better in the mouth than the barrel-water stored with us on the Ship. Yet I did my duty and filled the sacks, and dragged them back to the shore where others of the party stood in desolation, having found no wildfowl or yet good fish. Of plant-life there was little and no incentive for Botanizing.

As I gazed at the island it was as if some great creature with hot breath had flown above and scorched all below. Mr Pickersgill indicated that we should return to the Ship.

I am not certain how it began – only how it ended for that has been of more concern to me.

Our bags of barter lay on the shore when a group of the Natives attempted to seize some of them. Officer Edgecombe fired his musket, and the ball falling short did little to deter a second attempt on our stocks. The next fire shot dead a man, and the Natives moved threateningly towards our party, who retreated at great speed into the Sloop and pushed off, being under orders from Captain Cook to make no furious Encounter.

I would have been in the Longboat myself, except that I was standing like a beacon at the top of a mile-away hill.

I durst not call out for fear of drawing the Natives' wrath to myself, and I unarmed but for a knife and a cutlass. I dropp'd down flat, like a hare in a gale, and waited.

The squalls that had vexed us the night previous returned with renewed force, and I was obliged to retreat to what shelter the dismal island afforded. Yet I was comforted, as I crouched beneath a stark rock, that the weather would keep the Ship awhile and that my master Captain Cook would send a Party to remedy my absence. I wrapped myself in the provisions canvas I was carrying, and that kept me tolerably dry, and the weather being warm, and myself being young, I soon slept.

What lights are they that push against the eyes in sleep?

It was a cannon shot that woke me, the dawn rising yellow behind a curtain of rain. I got up from my shelter and scrambled back to the high point I had quitted, and looked out to sea. It was a dreadful sight. The Ship was sailing. In my agony I lost all care of my person and ran at pelt to the shore, waving my arms and calling. The petrels, thinking me of their kind, shrieked in return and widened their wings to welcome me. That was my companionship and I was fortunate of no other, for if the Natives had discovered me they may have revenged themselves on me for the dead man.

I half thought of swimming, but the waves were fierce and the Ship fast-tacking South with the wind. For what reason or purpose I had been left behind, I do not know, and it may be that there was no reason or purpose, for mankind must always be finding reasons where there are none, and comfort in a purpose that hardly exists.

So here I am, with nothing, at dawn, and the Ship like a thing dreamed from another star.

Up, Billy, up. There's none to save you now but your own self.

I began to search the island.

Hardly to be understood is the lack of vegetation.

I came to a deep pit, a quarry, worked by human hands and stone dug out from it and, from the tracks gouged into the earth, the stone dragged on sledges of some kind, but sledges made of what, and for what purpose and to what place, I could not tell.

Near at hand I found charcoal deposits, evidence of great and prolonged burning, and I took up a little of the charcoal to start myself a fire. Such a piece of work is man that although he must be about to die he will question his situation. The mystery of the pits and the burning did not bear upon my survival at all, or so I deemed, yet my mind was as eaten by curiosity as my flesh would be by maggots.

I heard a noise familiar to all seamen. Sure enough, scraping in the shallows of the dug pit were four or five small rats. I shouted and the things scurried away, one rolling a bird's Egg in his forefeet. I came to be uneasy then, for what in this barren place did a rat find for its contentment? The thought presented itself that it might be human remains that employed these creatures so busily. Yet my masters on the Ship had not spoke of Cannibals.

Happen this was a Ceremonial matter, and the dead put on pyres or burned here.

Yet I stayed uneasy.

And I had a thought of Lemon Curd.

If evidence was needed that man is nothing but a loose-tied sack of folly, seek no further than this my Billy-self. I am lost, abandoned, hungry, like to die, perched above a charnel-house, uneasy in all my thoughts, and neither the scriptures nor the words of Great Men present me any comfort, but the picture of a pot of Lemon Curd.

'God Forgive Me,' I say, and feel pity for a Deity that must concern Himself with pots of preserve. Had I lordship of the Universe I should roll men like marbles in the pan of space and never ask where they stopped or fell.

Here I am, stopped and fallen, this little round of life called a man.

Here I am, little Billy, and nothing round me but the sea.

What's that over there? Moving rapidly towards. Quick, Billy, slither slope-side and stalk it.

The Natives appear to be making procession towards some totem or obelisk, except that it is fringed. By use of my small telescope I discover, to my great surprise, that it is a tree, standing alone, and a genus of Palm. It may be that this is some rite of fertility to encourage the land to renew itself, such as we have seen on voyage in Tahiti.

A great cry goes up round the tree and what appears to be a dispute. Women, and this my first sight of them, are grouped against the men, mayhap as a part of the ritual, but one of the women is lying the length of her body against the tree, and wailing so strong that I can hear it from my Warren. A male figure, wearing a headdress of bird feathers, strikes the woman, and at this signal, for so I interpret it, all the women standing by are struck at by the males and driven away, as you would drive off a chatter of monkeys.

The men alone remain at the site and, to my surprise, two of the strongest in build step forward to fell the Palm.

While this strange matter is taking place, and I am ranging my Glass around and about the scene, I light upon a face that is not the face of a Native but the face of a European man, such as myself, yet older.

My excitement very nearly causes my discovery, as I stand to see him better, but at the very second the tree falls, and the noise of its crack is joined with the wailing of the women. The men take it up and away, bearing it on their shoulders, and very soon the site is empty, and after some short time I debate with myself that I can as well go forward as remain. I am to die, and may as well do so in the pursuit of some interest though it deliver no advantage.

At the stump of the tree there is evidence that this lonely specimen lately felled had been part of a grove or an area of forest. Yet if this dismal island had at some time boasted forests and groves, why had no pains been taken to maintain such as is needed for the minimum requirements of life?

I bethought me back to the Natives who had swarmed the Ship when we anchored a mile out. Their thievery had not been for iron stuff, in which they shewed scant interest, but wooden items of little value – discarded broom handles, broken splints, split barrels, wormy boards, a sea-sodden chest used for rope-ends. One of our men had obtained the promise of three virgins for the price of a breadboard. And yet, the breadboard given, the virgins had yet to be seen, and yet with Edgecombe's shot, it was all too late, too late.

But I am the one left behind, and if I could shrink my body to the size of my courage I would find the breadboard and make me a raft and never come back.

I gazed at the stump of the Palm. Why would a man destroy the very thing he most needs?

I followed the trail, easy to do, across the island, its grass so poor and thin that no sheep or goat could home there, and fowls must be pressed to scratch a living. The Natives themselves were not tall or numerous, and famine, I supposed, had kept them in check. I began to wonder what I should eat, and such am I that hunger seemed worse to me than death, and death by starvation far worse than death at a blow. I had in my bag two small bananas given by the Natives and a piece of dried meat brought from the Ship. My water-bottle was full but I had eaten nothing since yesterday night and I resolved to look for a settlement of some kind, reasoning that if a ceremony or rite was taking place, it would be left unguarded.

Reaching the top of the cliff, I looked out and, with my Glass, saw in the distance the last I would ever see of the *Resolution*: my knife and spoon in its pouch, my tankard on its hook, my clean shirt and breeches in a bundle in the corner of my hammock, my parrot that shouted, 'Billy-boy, Eyes Down', and my ration of rum, in other mouths. So be it. Life is all partings. James Hogan, First Mate. I loved him with the patience of an oyster longing for a pearl.

So be it.

Smoke below. The few huts we spied from the Ship are beneath me. Eyes down, the rest to follow; truly the eyes are the window of temptation. Tho' it must be said that there is small stuff here to tempt even the easiest pleased. The settlement is poor and without adornment, patched and shabby. A low charcoal fire burns in a ring of stones. A line of fishes is drying above it, fishes so modest that the scant smoke of the fire blows their tails backward and forward, as tho' they are trying to swim in their new element of air.

Swiftly, I stole the entire line and made off to consume them behind one of the huts. There I was, bones, heads, tails in my mouth like a dog, when a hand came from behind and seized my collar. I near enough choked to death, my heart pumping for terror, and when I looked up, there was a Native, brown and painted, a spear in his hand.

He took the fishes from me and speedily ate what remained. Then he prodded me forward, speaking I knew not what, and we set out, away from the settlement towards the shore, and towards the strange and silent stone idols we had sighted from the Ship.

I hardly know how to describe what I saw.

These Idols, staring out to sea with their massy stone faces, stood many feet high, dark and heavy and impassive, and seated upon great plinths of wood and stone. I could not fathom to myself how they had been carved by these Natives, nor how dragged to this place. I reasoned that the skill that could execute such design would shew other works: their dwellings would be more ingenious, their manner of living better considered. Where were their boats, their tackle, their meeting-houses?

I had little time to think on these things as I was pushed

forward in the circle of men, who soon had me stripped down to my breeches. My cutlass and knife and Glass were taken with much delight, and my coat and shirt and hat made the subject of great dispute among the Natives. It was all the power I had to keep my breeches, but I resolved to be murdered on the spot rather than be parted from them, for a man without breeches must either be a woman or an ass.

Out of sport or humour or the quick loss of purpose that is common among Natives, my tormentors let me alone as a group of children might do a puppy.

Looking about me for means of escape, it was then that I saw, at the base of the Idols, piles of human bones, like an open grave, and what courage remained to me leaked through the sieve of my terror.

As I stood, a Native came forward, his eyebrows and head shaved. Most curious were his fingernails, something above six inches long, and painted. The others seemed in awe and wonder at the man, and I guessed him to be a priest of the Idols. He made a sign, and two Natives came forward and roped my hands together, after which they pointed to a place a little way off, and I understood I was to walk there. At the spot, I sat down and my ankles were tied together. The Natives returned to the Idols and, to my great astonishment, joined together and began to rock the largest Idol at its base. To begin with I understood their actions as a form of worship, but as their labour increased, I saw that it was their intention to shatter the Idol on the ground.

My mind was dizzy from the sun and from fear. Such prodigious labour as had been employed to make such a thing could surely not be wasted in its shattering?

It must be that others, not of this island, had at some time imposed their gods on the Natives, and this was the people's revenge.

As I sat, the Idol began to topple, and the earth to shake under me. There was a crack like a splitting-axe at a rotten tree, and the blind stone god fell face to the ground. The sea-waves washed at its ruin.

There was silence among the Natives. Then, into the space between one moment and the next, a man in a white feather headdress, his person decorated about with white feathers, ran forward along the sands, followed by others, waving spears and shouting in a mixed and boiling broth of rage and pain.

At once the two parties fell to fighting, using the slain mountain of the Idol as a kind of barricade on both sides. I could do nothing, and nothing I did do until, with a great cry, the Native with the talons seemed to order his men to desert the scene. As the battle ended, this Bird Man drew with his nails some sign on the Stone God and, appearing to fear no further reprisal, turned his back on his foes and made away.

The rival chief, for so I thought him, walked slowly to the thing of stone, lying like a whale that has lost the sea, and inspected the sign. Then he shook his head, and began to walk backwards, away from the Idol.

As I watched, my nostrils twitched with smoke, and I looked towards the settlement. The great plumes of smoke I saw were not made by a charcoal fire for smoking fishes. It must be that the few huts were on fire. This, then, was the reason for the sudden retreat of the Bird Man and his followers: they were burning the village.

All at once I was alone. The great noise and commotion

and effort of the passing few hours was done. It was as tho' I did not exist. Perhaps I had been forgotten, perhaps left to die as a sacrifice to a fallen Idol, or to the power that had destroyed it.

I hopped up on my feet and jumped both feet together down towards the sea, a puny, pitiful, tied thing, no better than a cat in a sack. I looked out across the Ocean, and determined to drown myself.

I was up to my chin when the shout came, and I will never forget it. Never. For it seems to me that any hope in life is such a shout; a voice that answers the silent place of despair. It is silence that most needs an answering — when I can no longer speak, hear me.

I turned.

Him that I had spied through my Glass was waving at me from the shore. He quickly waded and swam and came near me, and I would hazard that he was a man of forty years, yet wonderfully preserved, lean and strong, and with a cheerful, inquisitive face that reminded me of a good dog that never had a bad master. He smiled, and his teeth were white and whole. 'English man,' he said, pointing at me, and I surely would have drowned in astonishment, had he not caught me and quickly untied my wrists, then dived down into the water and untied my legs. He slapped my bare shoulders, and made that we should wade back to the shore.

As we came near the Idol, he paused and looked sorrowful. 'Dead,' he said, giving me cause to think that he was more a Native than a European man.

He took my hand, and ran with me about a mile along the sand until we came to a honeycomb of caves low in the cliff. A simple canoe was pulled outside one of these.

He took me inside the cave and embraced me, and I could feel straight away that he was eager of a reward for his pains. I put my hand down to where he was stiff and soon had him tidy and soft again, for I am used to such things from the Ships, and it means little to me to steady a man. He made to handle me in return, but I shook my head. I was weak and fearful out of all that had passed, and wanted rest.

My companion soon made a small fire of charcoal and dried seaweed and began to roast a seabird.

'Spikkers,' he said, pointing at his own chest. 'Roggeweins' Ship.'

His English was poor, but it was English nonetheless, and I discovered that his father had landed at Easter Island with the Dutch Captain Roggeweins in 1722. As far as I could understand it, his father had deserted the vessel and remained on the island with one of the women. By sign he shewed me that his parents were now dead, and that all his brothers and sisters were dead, for want of food or in some conflict. His father had taught him Dutch, Spanish and some English. His only wish was to escape the island and settle in his father's great sailing city – Amsterdam, 'much wood, many houses'.

I had visited Amsterdam myself, and I described to him the wonders of that city: its canals, its bridges, its tall houses with their hoists for hauling merchandise. I told of its burghers and its matrons, of its warehouses piled with grain, of its trade with the Indies, splendid and jewelled, of an elephant I had seen – tho' the elephant was difficult to describe so that I was obliged to draw it crudely on the cave wall in charcoal.

'And its trunk,' I said, 'can lift a man six feet nearer to God.'

When I said 'God', Spikkers went to the back of the cave and pulled out a wooden box. 'Wood,' he said, bowing to the box.

I saw at once it was a Bible box and, sure enough, inside were three Bibles; one written in Dutch, one in Spanish, and the King James.

'Read,' he said.

I opened the Bible. 'In the beginning, God created the Heavens and the Earth, and the Earth was without Form and Void, and darkness moved on the face of the Deep.'

'MakeMake build the world, and this the world,' said Spikkers, pointing round and down, by which I had to guess he meant the island. 'Out There, after the sea, Hiva, where the Living go, and Po, where the Dead go.'

'Where is Amsterdam?' I asked, for sake of play.

Spikkers nodded, certain that he knew the answer to that, and when it grew dark, he led me outside the cave and shewed me to lie down beside him.

'My father lies on earth, this so, and he tells me his dreams. When he has made much dreaming, he points to his home.'

Spikkers pointed up to a bright and steady star close to the moon. With his other hand he held mine and kissed it. 'Holland,' he said, kissing my fingers, one by one by one by one, and until my hand became a five-pointed star.

And the *Resolution*, and Plymouth, and my mother's house dock-side at Chatham, and the Green Dragon that sells oysters and whitebait, and the barrels of rum waiting to be loaded, and the boys that would stow away in a bale of cloth, and the stories as long as a two-year voyage South, and the last meal of fresh beef and onions, and the cheers from the town, and the flag up, and the people waving

waving smaller smaller, and the smell of casked apples and the last sight of a known shore and, faintly, the sound of a Church bell, are these things nearer than a Holland star – or easier to believe?

When day came, I attempted to discover the meaning of what I had seen with the Idol. Spikkers grew in agitation and, with gestures and broken English, explained, or so I think, that the island had two leaders, at bitter war – the Bird Man and the White Man. The White Man, called the Ariki Mau, was the pale Native dressed in feathers, the priest-man with supernatural powers who was able to fly with the Dead, and bring visions to the Living. The islanders still revered him, but they feared more the Bird Man, with his shaved brows and head and his talon-fingers. The Bird Man had control of a kind of army, and ruled the island with this mob. Food was scarce, and the best of everything went first to the Bird Man to favour among his followers.

And the Idols?

Spikkers moaned and covered his face with his hands, and rocked on his heels like one abandoned to grief. 'Mana gone,' he said. 'They kill the Mo'ai to kill the Mana.'

It does seem that the Easter Islanders practised a form of ancestor worship, and that it was they, indeed, and not another people who had laboured to quarry and raise the statues. Spikkers spoke of a 'back-time' when the labouring of the Stone Gods had been the sole purpose of the island's society, and when the carvers and workers were fed and clothed by the other islanders.

I fancied that this statue building was intended to obtain supernatural rewards, not dissimilar to our own medieval cathedrals, and paid for in the same manner, for a man who is building a Church cannot sow oats and barley or tend his flock, but must rely on others to supply his dinner.

And I thought of the immense human effort that is put to enterprises of all kinds that yield no obvious return and yet are deemed more worthy than the grazing of oxen and the manufacture of cloth.

I do not deem this a fault. There must be some part of Man that is more than his daily round. Some part of him that will use his profit on a matter of no profit, for the Bible says to us, 'What should it profit a Man that he gain the whole World and lose his own Soul?'

But none has seen his Soul, yet all have seen a small corner of the world, and would have more of it.

It was the day of our Departure from Plymouth Sound, that being the 13th of July 1772 and the weather clowdy.

The Ship was well furnished with mutton and good victuals of every kind, and brandywine and portwine.

It was our purpose to discover the Southern Continent, if such a place there be, and to make a Map, and to claim Land for the Crown. Yet there are at once two voyages to be made – the first of direction and course, and the second unpurposed and untried, and if that voyage can be mapped I do not know any man that has mapped it, for each must make the voyage his own, and record it in the secret places of his heart.

I do not know if Man has a Soul, but if he does, then it follows in the wake of his Ship, like an albatross or frigate-bird. I do not believe that he carries it within him like a shadowy shape of himself inside himself, and that is the reason his Soul is nowhere to be found at death, for it does not keep its residence in a man's body, but in his purpose. As I go forward my Soul comes after me to see what it is that I do, for there is a curiosity there, like that of a seabird, that ploughs the wake of a Ship and then flies away no man knows where.

The Ship, the Crew, the Voyage, and what am I but a Ship in little, and above me the white throat of a winged bird?

I was now satisfied in my mind that the Idols had been worked for magical purposes and in veneration of unseen powers. Rival wars had begun the deadly destruction of vying Idols – for if I can keep my ancestor, while losing you yours, I increase my Mana. The waste of such an enterprise seems hardly to have struck them, but I admit that my countrymen do the same in their warring and burning. Mankind, I hazard, wherever found, Civilized or Savage, cannot keep to any purpose for much length of time, except the purpose of destroying himself.

Spikkers took my hand and walked with me back round the island towards the site of the felling of the tree. I was as much vexed by that as I had been by the Idols, and urged him to make an explanation.

It was a ghastly history.

In 'back-time', the god MakeMake had filled the island with forests and springs and fishes and birds so that no man could want who could stretch out his hand. Into this abundance came the Ancestors in boats, making houses and ceremonial dwellings and living only by the word of the White Man – the Ariki Mau.

Wood was needed for fires and building, and land was needed for plantains and bananas and sundry crops. The Palms that were so tight together that a man must walk sideways to pass through them were felled, one by one by one, until, slow by slow by slow, the seabirds no longer visited the island, and the rain no longer fell, and the ground crumbled and burned, and the soil turned to red dust that grew nothing.

Yet I was perplexed by this, for a man must need a mighty number of fires to clear a forest, and the Islanders did not seem so many that they could use up a whole world. Happen it was the rats that had eaten the nuts of the Palm and harmed its generation – we had seen infestations of rat-kind in Tahiti – yet the natives there had managed their land with broad sense.

Spikkers pointed to the Idols, and mimed to me that the great stones must be pulled from the quarry on wooden sledges, and that entire Palms must be used as raft-lengths to float the stone down the coast, and that the kiln-work and the carving-work required ever greater amounts of wood, and no man dreamed that the wood gone would never return.

'And this tree yesterday that I saw drop, was it the last tree of them all?'

Spikkers nodded his head. The Ariki Mau had ordered its protection as a sacred tree, and the Bird Man had ordered its felling.

'Is it to be believed,' I said, 'that an island abundant in all things necessary has been levelled to this wasteland through the making of a Stone God and then by his destruction?'

Spikkers nodded his head.

In the days that followed he made me to visit the South and West of the island, and truly all that he had spoken had its truth in the deadened land and the eerie sight of the stone Mo'ai – some remaining upright, their smooth backs to the sea, their unseeing eyes fixed on the inland, and countless more felled in savage attacks on their purpose.

To the East of the island we did not venture, for that part, said Spikkers, is home to the Bird Man and his followers, and a place of utmost danger to us.

I began to understand that Spikkers was preparing for some conquest of his own.

He had revealed to me that the Bird Man's reign lasted for only twelve moons, making it a little less than a Solar year, and that every year, at the appointed time, there was a competition, or some manner of sport, that decided the winner or leader of the Bird Man cult for the year to come.

I tried not to laugh at his serious description, and half thought that I had misfathomed his explanation, for the thing seemed to be an Egg Race – and the one who could gather the first Egg laid by the visiting Sooty Terns would claim for himself the privileges of the Bird Man.

'Tis not strange that the Bird be such a symbol for the Natives, for the Bird may travel where he will, across the sea to other lands, and the Natives make no distinction between the lands of the Dead and the lands of the Living. That they themselves cannot travel at all, having not even a piece of wood remaining with which to fashion a deep-sea canoe, lends the Bird an increase of power. The Bird that flies, and the man that cannot, lies at the bottom of all their thoughts.

And Spikkers would have me know that birds were once abundant here, like fishes and trees and water, and their departure is the anger of the gods.

Spikkers is no friend of the Bird Man: he worships the old way of Ariki Mau, and has formed a plan to win back for the old gods the rights of the new power.

He shall climb the cliffs and find the Egg and give it to the Ariki Mau, so that once more the power of the island lies in one place. This, he said, will end the destruction and the civil war and bring peace and prosperity to the island. The trees will grow and the birds will return.

He does believe this, truly, and his shining face causes me to drop my eyes for fear of hurting his happiness.

He shows me the cliffs where the Terns will come, as high and impossible as a moon landing, and he shows me a chart, hidden in his cave, where he has scratched the calendar of their flights over many years – or moons, as he understands time. He is made ready, and for his reward, he says, he will ask only to leave the island with me when the next Ship sails this way. I do not say to him that I have no hope of such a Ship.

There are many things I do not say.

In the back of the cave is a piece of blue cloth. Wrapped in the piece of blue cloth is a Delft tile. The tile is a picture of a tall house with its door open. A man in a hat waits inside the hall.

It is six month since I found myself abandoned here, as foolish as a dog that leaps from the deck in some stray port.

Through these six month I have lived in Spikkers' cave, and he has fed me and made much of me and kept the rest at bay, for he has authority of some sort with the Ariki Mau in that he has learned writing, which imparts ceremonial power. This script, which they name Rongorongo, does not use our alphabet, yet rather forms characters and signs that stand in place of whole phrases or expressions. This powerful Mana is translated on to spears and holy objects, and is now employed for the Egg Race, for so I shall call it, as servants of the Ariki Mau begin to gather beneath the cliffs, waving flags to attract the Tern.

This is a magical observance, but not so strange to me

for mine own country uses a flag as its symbol, which it waves to attract attention and to signify dominion. The Land we claim for our own we claim by flag, and why should not these Natives do the same, except that the territory they desire be a spiritual holding?

It is as if, here, everything signifies some other thing: the Bird, the Egg, the flag, the writing, the winning, the winner, the Stone Gods, even the island, even the world are symbols for what they are not.

I have a sixpence in my pocket and a pair of trousers that allows me to have a pocket. I was a seaman and I had a mother. Bundle it all together and what does it stand for? Is it that I am Nothing that I must always stand for Something? Six month have passed and I cling to my Self as an Englishman, as I clung to my trousers on the sands when they made fain to undress me.

I must have some covering, the world must have some covering for its nakedness, and so the simplest things come to impart the greatest significance – a piece of bread becomes a body, a sip of wine, my life's blood. That one thing should stand for another is no harm, until the thing itself loses any meaning of its own. The island trees and all of this good land were sacrificed to a meaning that has now become meaningless. To build the Stone Gods, the island has been destroyed, and now the Stone Gods are themselves destroyed.

It is the day of the Race.

The Tern has been sighted.

The cliff face is sheer as Judgement Day. Myself, I could not climb it to save my Soul, but if I am right-minded that our Souls are Birds, they will have gone before us to that high place, and have no more use for bodies like mine.

The cliff-stone is like a puzzle – where now for fingers and feet?

I count twenty-three of the Natives running for the honour of the prize, and none thinks he will fail. The Bird Man clan has picked a proxy for the Race, a swaggering oaf who will win the Egg for his master, or so he believes.

And I think to myself that I could as well be on the dock-side at Chatham for all the vanity and preening that I see before me. This may be a wasteland but here, as in every place the world can shew, men will gamble and plot and fight and fall, all for the winning of a trophy. A woman's heart, a piece of land, a kingdom, a lordship, a contract, a ship, an egg – it hardly matters the which or the what, as soon as it is seen to be desired by one, another will make a prize of it.

Spikkers, clad in my trousers to bring him luck – or, as he calls it, to add my Mana to his own – bends his head so that I can tie his head-band. He has sewn a pouch to the front of it, and in the manner of the Kangaroos will carry the Egg in that pouch. He tells me he has had a dream, and that his father came to him and gave him the Egg in one hand, and with the other hand took him to live in Amsterdam, in a house, he says, made all of wood, and him the richest man on the earth.

It is sure that here their word for wood – '*rakau*' – also means 'riches', and that if they were, this day, to find a mine of gold or a cave of rubies, they would account it as nothing against a wormy plank washed up by the sea.

The signal given, the competitors begin their run and climb – some with crude home-made pegs hung round their waists to cram into the rock for a foothold, and some with human bones strapped to their forearms as levers or grips.

Near all the people of the island have turned forth to watch the Race, and there is great shouting and cheering among the rivals, as at a cockfight.

Up they go, fast as rats.

And my heart is beating.

Truth tell, anywhere is a life, once there is a love.

I took to sea in that I could not stay at home, in that I could not stay at home for James Hogan had took to sea.

Now that I have Nothing and am Nothing, I have shrunk this pod of an island further and made our cave an everywhere. When everywhere is here there is no further to travel, and tho' I have flung out my message in a bottle, I care nothing if the world catches my signal or no, and tho' I scan the seas for a ship, I care nothing that it come or no, and have employed myself with yams and Wells and small fish, and wait for him who rescued me.

Where is he?

I waded into the sea and swam round the point. There was Spikkers, high, higher than any, and climbing towards the sun like a god. Above him the Tern swooped and flew, her agitation betraying her. I saw him pause, reach, find. I saw the jubilation in his body, the way a fox is jubilant when it takes a rabbit – its very blood and bone caught rejoicing, his back stiff with pleasure.

I saw him pack the Egg into his headband, and begin his descent, quick and clean as rain over the rock-face, moving down and down towards success.

And then, him still high, and a light wind rippling him, I saw his rival, the oaf, grabbing his way round the cliff with heavy hands, dislodging rocks with his feet like paddles, and

I saw him meet a ledge and crouch on it, and as Spikkers came down, light and quiet as a new beginning, this oaf grabbed him by the back of the neck and took the Egg.

I cried out, but the wind tore my voice away, and if either man heard me, he gave no sign. Spikkers struggled and fought, but the lightness of his body and his quick strength were no match for the brute who seized him above his head and dashed him over the cliff.

And in the air a body falling. And in the air a body falling like a star. And in the air a body falling like a star out of its orbit. And in the air a body falling like a star out of its orbit and coming to earth and seen no more.

I swam to him and lifted him from the rock into the sea and towed his limp body round the coast to the shore of our cave and carried him out of the water.

I broke his Bible box into bits and lit a fire and laid his body beside it and felt where the bones were broken in his back and chest and legs and licked the blood from his mouth and tried to give him my breath and I would have given him one of my legs and one of my arms and one of my kidneys and half of my liver and four pints of my blood and all easy for I had already given him my heart.

Do not die.

Night comes long and straight and his breath comes in shorter bursts like an animal that has run too far.

In the sky there is a star called Holland and the tall wooden houses of Amsterdam are clear to be seen.

'*In my dream,*' he says, 'the island is thick-forested like fur, and green and dark and alive. The waterfalls flow again and there is a lake as hidden as sleep. *Where are we going, Billy?* he says.

To him I say, 'We are coming by Ship to the Amstel River, and look at us now with bales of cloth and a palm tree in a barrel. A canal-boat will take us along the Singel and stop us at a house where the door is open.' I held up the Delft tile, like a mirror to his face.

He smiled.

'Go in,' I say to him. 'Go in.'

And he passes through the door. And in the house he must make ready till I have finished my business here and come back to him.

A white Bird opens its wings.

Post-3War

I was travelling home on the Tube tonight and I noticed that someone had left a pile of paper on the seat opposite. It was late, I was a bit drunk, a bit bored, a bit restless, so I swung across the centre gap from one bum-soiled seat to another and carefully shifted the bundle on to my knees. It was yellow, pre-war, you don't see much paper these days, maybe scrap, maybe rubbish, maybe old instruction manuals translated into English from the Japanese.

The Stone Gods, said the title. OK, must be anthropology. Some thesis, some PhD. What's that place with the statues? Easter Island?

I flicked through it. No point starting at the beginning – nobody ever does. Reading at random is better: maybe hit the sex scenes straight away.

At night in the belly of the Ship, I lay beside Spike and thought how strange it was to lie beside a living thing that did not breathe.

A love story, that's what it is – maybe about aliens. I hate science fiction.

There's a name and address on the front page. I wonder if there'll be a reward? Or is that just for cats and dogs?

★

I had another look: *Everything is imprinted for ever with what it once was.*

Is that true?

This is the story of my life. Before I was born, curled up like a universe waiting to happen, my mother heard that my father was not going to marry her. It was too late to do anything about me: I was coming, ready or not, and whatever I was, I was there. She was going to give birth.

My grandmother believed in Trial by Baby. Take the thing in your arms and go from door to door until someone says yes.

They had no television, no phone, no car. They hadn't been long off rationing. The streets where they lived were a junk-yard of bomb damage and scrap. I was born on a metal-framed bed, horsehair mattress, spring coils, so much blood they had to burn the sheet. But I was born, and nothing anyone can do about that.

My advice to anyone is, 'Get born.'

So here I come, turning like a skydiver, head first, my skull soft and open where the stars come in, and one star just visible like the bud of a horn. Here I am, using the edge of the star like a laser to cut through the tissue of the uterus, a light-edged baby into a star-cut world.

The bed broke. The springs in the middle had been tied together with fencing wire. It snapped. My mother folded in half, and I was pulled out like a calf from under her. Don't cut the cord: get some fencing wire and tie me to her.

The line that fed me, the line that breathed me, the line that tapped messages from the world outside, the line that was a tightrope between her fear and my joy, the line I would have to cross, some day, and never come back. The line that is the first line of this story – *I was born*. The line that had nothing to read between it – being only one, one only, my lifeline.

Cut it.

My grandmother cut the cord with her teeth. Her teeth were false and the greasy, bloody umbilical cord caught in her top plate and pulled it out. She went to soak it in Steradent and left my mother to her first milking.

Joy. I wanted to be born. I wanted to be here. Fear. She didn't know what to do next. She was young, seventeen. My grandmother was not yet forty. But it was a different world then because the world is always remaking itself, and after the war there was a lot of remaking to be done. I was born in the ashes of the fire, and I learned how to burn.

I remember reading that Samuel Beckett remembered life in the womb. Everyone believes him because he won the Nobel Prize; I doubt that anyone will believe me, or if they do they won't understand that it's possible to be telling the truth even in the moment of invention.

I remember my mother telling my grandmother that she wanted to make a new life. They'd been going to Ireland on a boat, her and my dad, but now he was going and she wasn't, and she said she couldn't sit at home and look after me. I was knocking on her stomach wall trying to be heard – '*Don't stay at home! We can go together. I don't eat much.*' She didn't hear me.

She was frying bacon in a burned pan on the gas stove. I was pressed against the slot where the grill pan goes. There's not much room in there, unless you're a grill pan.

145

I can see why no one wants to spend their life in front of an oven.

We did mopping and washing. She was tired. We went to sleep under the quilt, and it was the last night that I would ever spend inside her. *Keep me in the mop bucket or the slot where the grill pan goes, but don't let me go because I love you.*

Love without thought. Love without conditions. Love without promises. Love without threats. Love without fear. Love without limits. Love without end.

I think she did love me, for a minute, for a second, for the time it takes to remember, for the time it takes to forget. We had twenty-eight days together and then I was gone.

My grandmother went up and down the streets, and it would have been easier to give away a rabbit or a chicken. 'Nobody wants it,' she said, but that wasn't true: the one person who wanted it was the one person it wanted too.

We slept in the same bed; there was no other. They wound the gaping spring round a bit of wood and jammed a broom across the frame. My father said he'd marry my mother if she gave the baby away. Then they could start again. Then they could have a new life. But I was a new life.

It was a long time ago.

– I was born in the year 1632 in the city of York, of a good family, tho' not of that country . . .

That's not me, that's Robinson Crusoe. Birth is a shipwreck, the mewling infant shored on unknown land. My mother's body split open and I was the cargo for salvage.

I suppose you have to believe there is something worth salvaging; and with me it seems that nobody did.

There are so many stories of barrels and pots and chests and trunks that haul up on to the beach, and they may contain treasure, or they may be spoiled, or they may be just ballast and rocks. The trouble with babies is that they are made like a safe – no way to see what's inside and no guarantee that the effort will be worth the trouble. Spin the numbers, crack the code, but the door won't swing open. Babies are safes on a time-delay. It takes years for the door to swing open, and even when it does, the best minds are undecided as to the value of the contents.

And to make life more difficult, babies who come as treasure bring with them their own magician. Open the box and it may be empty. What's inside may already have been spirited away. By the time you get to it there may be nothing there. Rot? Evaporation? A vanishing trick? Are all those empty adults born so? Or did something happen in the box?

There I was, sealed and locked, chances of a piece of gold inside me as chancy as tapping a barrel of rum. The seawater gets inside, life is easily adulterated. Only in stories does the thing come out fortunate and clean, gifted and golden. But there's another story within that story – the toad, the beggar, the silted-up well, the pigsty, the stinking sludge, the dark cave, the wounded deer, the forest where nothing grows. The buried treasure is really there, but it is buried.

Here I am, arms and legs like handles and levers. Open me if you can. Carry me off. Take me with you.

This new world weighs a yatto-gram.

★

Shipwrecked on the shore of humankind, the baby can only hope that someone will keep it until it is old enough to keep itself. That didn't happen to me. My mother had the doctor in and he filled in a certificate in flowing blue fountain pen that said I was healthy and normal and that there was no reason why I should not be adopted.

My grandmother took this piece of paper with her on her rounds, hoping that bright eyes and no infectious diseases would persuade a gambler to try their luck. But the initial investment was high – feed it, clothe it, send it to school, and it might turn out rotten, after all.

At night, coming back from my visits round the world, my mother was there, worn and anxious, but I didn't know those words, 'worn', 'anxious', I knew only that she cried and then I cried too, not for wet or hunger but for the fear that was slowly darkening the joy, the way a shadow crosses the floor.

There are things that you can do with a baby you can't keep. You can set off one day and come home without her because she can't scent her way back like a dog, or make her way home over the rooftops like a cat. Wrap her up well and put her down and there she stays, wailing till some passer-by might take her up out of pity.

My mother set off. We went for a walk. A bonfire gone out but warm in the ashes was burning on the edge of a derelict street. She laid me gently in the ashes to save me getting cold, and went away.

She walked for two hours and came back. I was asleep. She picked me out of the cinders and we went home.

There were other attempts: the conductor saw what she'd done and made the bus driver turn off-route, right round and behind her, and the conductor stood on the open platform, me in his arms, with the bus going at walking pace, in the wrong direction, and me the size of a sardine, watching the shine on the badge of his hat.

She's walking along, crying, trying not to look, then the conductor pulls her up on to the platform with one hand, and sits her on the torn leather bench seat at the back, and plunges his hand into the bag of coppers and sixpences that is the fare money, and just gives her a handful, there and then, breaking open his ticket machine so that the bus company won't know what he's done. She takes the money. She takes me. She goes home.

Love is not easy to leave behind.

The doctor comes back. This place is unsanitary, bleak, damp; the mother's health is at stake. The baby has a weak chest. No good under the quilt on the broken bed. There's a place the baby can go, and soon some new parents can be found. It will be better. Better to begin again. This time she won't have to leave me and falter. This time someone will take me away, and they won't bring me back. You don't know that, when you're a baby. You go with them, you go with anybody, and for a little while, it's all right, but there's only one face, only one smell, only one voice. Where is she?

You never stop looking. That's what I found, though it took me years to know that's what I've been doing. The person whose body I was, whose body was me, vanished after twenty-eight days. I live in an echo of another life.

It's like one of those shells with the sea inside it. Not every day, not often, but put it to your ear and the other life is still there.

I can hear you – the tide in, out. The rush of water across the pebbles.

Pass me the screwdriver.

So there I was, like a piece of flat-pack furniture, dismantled in one home, re-erected in another. Unfortunately for all my parents, previous and current, the assembly instructions had been translated into English from Japanese.

When I was gone, my mother came running down the street after me. Look at her, like an angel, like a light-beam, running alongside the pram. I lifted up my hands to catch her, and the light was there, the outline of her, but like angels and light she vanished, and it was nearly the last time, but not yet.
 Is that her, at the end of the street, smaller and smaller, like a light-years-away star?

I always believed that I would see her again.

El Dorado, Atlantis, the Gold Coast, Newfoundland, Plymouth Rock, Rapanaui, Utopia, Planet Blue. Chanc'd upon, spied through a glass darkly, drunken stories strapped to a barrel of rum, shipwreck, a Bible Compass, a giant fish led us there, a storm whirled us to this isle. In the wilderness of space, we found . . .

The lost and found/found and lost is like a section of our DNA. In the spiral of us is the story we can't tell – the story we tell in single lines, separated from one another not by neat spaces but by torn-out years.

Emerson said that the rarest thing on the planet is a truly individual action – but I'd set the bar at a story told. It's why the nineteenth-century writers favoured such long and satisfyingly plotted novels. Some of them – like George Eliot – really believed there was something to tell and that we could tell it. Dickens knew very well that we could not, but he told it anyway, glittering and bravura. It's one way of defying chaos – the kind of Chaos, with a capital C, that can't be avoided; the exuberant, unfolding, unpredictable universe, expanding when it should be contracting, made largely of something that is not something but nothing – dark energy, anti-matter. A thing unconfined. What to say when the certainties fail?

Words are the part of silence that can be spoken.

Her voice was low, strongly accented, Lancashire. A voice made out of hills shuttered up low under the sky and ribbed with dry-stone walls, stone nearly black from the mills.

Her voice was made out of the mills, too, Manchester cottons, jacquard and coarse weave. Looms as wide as the fortunes they made. Looms that ran racket enough to drown the drone of the bombers. No use shouting. Use both hands dancing like two creatures mating. They all did it, and at the same time spoke the words they conjured from their fingers, as though the words came out of their fingers and palms like card tricks.

'I'm going to have a baby . . .'

Spring me out of both your hands, Ace of Clubs, but I never wanted to be the cosh that hurt you.

It's risky but it could work. It's our only chance.

*

My father was a gambler – what else can you be when you live without any hope of the world? Chance is just that – a chance – and the cards offer better odds than the factory.

He won a packet. He was drinking in the pub. My mother was working extra to save for a winter coat. It was already November.

The next day he waited for her after work and took her to a fancy shop with mannequins in the window – all wearing winter coats.

'Sort thwon thi wants,' he said, seducing her with wool like a merchant on a sheep road, and perhaps he had been that once, when the Pennines were wool and wood, before the industrial revolution of cotton and coal.

He wrapped her in a coat, then he wrapped her in his arms. They went to a boarding-house that sat in a hill-cleft, and he told the woman who fed them hotpot and tea that they were man and wife. And for a night they were.

My father was soon spent up and back in the factory. My mother returned to the mill. By Christmas she knew she was pregnant, and when my grandmother gave her a swirling drink that tasted of aloes and smelled of death, she went into the yard to drink it and emptied it down the toilet.

On I went, into the freezing cold of January, safe under my mother's woollen coat.

She is all States, all princes I, Nothing else is . . .

At liberty in my mother's kingdom, at sail on amniotic seas, harm was not anything that could happen to me. She did what she could – she gave me a chance at life, as good a gamble as my father took, and perhaps it would pay off.

Twice turned out — once from the womb-world, once from her, and for ever — banishment became its narrative equivalent, a story I could tell. But because of this I know that inside the story told is the story that cannot be told. Every word written is a net to catch the word that has escaped.

It's late. I am on the Tube, reading a lost manuscript. I am a lost manuscript, surfacing in fragments, like a message in a bottle, a page here, a page there, out towards an unknown shore. It has been the same all my life because my mother set the numbers that way, coded me, programmed me, and although it is possible to play with the numbers, I can't break the shape. Determinism versus Freewill is a false study — unhelpful, a time-waster. Life has never been All or Nothing — it's All and Nothing. Forget the binaries.

So, am I blaming my mother? No. There's no one to blame, no one to hold responsible unless they take responsibility. I am responsible for myself, and I was from the moment they came with the pram and the blanket.

Goodbye, then . . .

Nobody we knew had a car. Not the woman from the Adoption Society. She wrapped me up, put me into the pram, and off we went, and that night for the first night, I was alone.

Night twenty-nine of my whole life.

Twenty-nine — a room number, a lucky charm, a winning horse, a marriageable age, the number of months it takes Saturn to orbit the sun. Saturn, planet of leadwork and limitation, child-eater, ruler of Capricorn.

★

On night thirty-two my mother came home from the mill and made a detour round the gasworks to the Adoption Society. She found a foothold in the back wall and hauled herself up, goat-style, to stand on top of the coping slabs and look in through the window. There were several cots, high-sided and severe.

She stood like a lighthouse, like a pulsar, and I was a radio telescope that caught the signal. There she is, a star the size of a city, pulsing through the universe with burned-out energy. I know you're there, I know where you are, I can track you because we are the same stuff.

She heard me crying, like a cat knows its kitten, but she couldn't grab me by the scruff and haul my legs out over the wall and away. I tried to get up but had no muscles to do it. A four-week kitten could have crawled towards her, but not me. She was too far away for me to see with the naked eye, or touch with the naked body, skin on skin, like a graft. I lay, she left, and what happened that night, I don't know, but the night after, they closed the curtains at the window. But curtains, windows, walls make no difference to what can be transmitted and what can be received.

Moon like a china globe, pendent globe-light in the room like a china moon, and my burned-out mother signalling in our private sky.

Is this how it ends?
It isn't ended yet.

I know she came back to change her mind, but it was too late, because she had signed the papers, and although manuscripts get lost as readily as children, official papers hold fast their dull and damaging life. What's best to throw away? The paperwork or the love? It's in the best interests of the child – but how do they know that, or the meaning of any of those separate words? Best. Interest. Child.

A lost world. A traveller's tale. Drunken stories strapped to a barrel of rum. A seabird, a space-ship, a signal, speed of light. A shooting star. Another life. Long gone.

My mother was born in World War Two.

My grandfather came home on leave and got into the soggy bed with my grandmother, and found an hour that wasn't made of mud and bayonets. And so my mother arrived to the bombing of 1943, and grew up wearing one dress with one knitted jumper over the top. She was small and strong and red; a red tree in a dark wood.

In the wind and cold, and the sometimes sun, thankful for the sun on the stone of the houses, a place to warm your back, a place to lean, she leaned and looked out past the mills to the hills, the Pennines that held the towns like a memory. She walked out, long walks past abandoned farms and scattered ordnance, the remains of the war, uncleared, left for moss to grow on the anti-aircraft guns, and silted earth to fill the trenches. She walked out till she could look back on the city, with its dirty clouds and smoking chimneys, and she marvelled that that was her life because up here, where it was windy and clean, it didn't feel like her life. She believed she could walk on and away, turn her back, begin again. Later, when I was walking inside her, I believed it too.

There was a place we used to go – her walking on the outside, me walking on the inside, weight-free, like a spaceman.

There's a track, there's a stream. The track rises steeply

– I can feel it by her breathing. The stream has watercress growing in the fast parts – she bends and eats it sometimes so she won't be anaemic. When she does that, everything inside goes green.

At the bend in the track, she pauses. She loves the house ahead – an old stone farmhouse, built on the drop to the stream; she drinks from the water barrel by the front door. She looks carefully at the fruits forming on the apple tree. There's a gate between the house and the track, and we lean on the gate very often, and she says, 'This is our house,' and I can smell the woodsmoke from the fire.

Freedom. Walk a little further on. Freedom.

World War Two. Another war to end all wars. Freedom.

And then . . .

Identity cards. Tracking devices in vehicles. Compulsory fingerprint database. Guilty until proven innocent. No right of appeal for convicted terrorists. Thirty billion pounds for new-generation Trident. Diplomatic-style immunity from investigation and prosecution for all elected politicians. Stop and Search. Police powers of arrest extended to 'reason to believe . . .' End of dual citizenship. Curfew Zones. Routine military patrols in 'areas of tension'. CCTV on every street. CCTV compulsory in mosques. Chip implants for prisoners on probation and for young offenders. No demonstrations, on-line protests shut down, those responsible cautioned. New Public Order laws, the Freedom Act, to be signed by all citizens and including the requirement to 'report any person or persons who are or who appear to be acting contrary to the rights and responsibilities of ordinary citizens as outlined in the Act'. Right to enter homes and businesses without a warrant.

★

To distract from all this, the Government built a super-casino in every city, licensed twenty-four-hour drinking, legalized prostitution and lowered the Age of Consent to fourteen. This was to show that we were secular and tolerant, not bigoted and fanatical.

The Prime Minister made a speech: serious threat – forty-five minutes to destruction, rallying cry like 1939, but this would be a peaceful war, liberate our fellow citizens across the world, freedom war, air-strike war, no nuclear threat. China, Iran, Pakistan. China, Iran, Pakistan. And a picture on the late news of children stretched like a journey across time – except there was no more time. They were dead.

The USA allocated $650 billion to the Pentagon. More than the defence budget of every other country in the world put together.

There was a polar bear stranded on an ice-floe. There were hurricanes, flooding, melting, landslides. There were rows about carbon quotas, carbon capture, carbon trading, as though the carbon footprint was just a matter of dropping a shoe size.

The Pope went mad and appeared in a bonnet to tell the world that the Antichrist was going to return as a peace-loving eco-warrior, ushering in a new kind of Paganism, nature versus the spirit. Catholics were instructed to abandon Green politics and prepare for Holy War.

In America a different kind of religious extremism, committed to Armageddon, liked the idea of the Antichrist appearing as a planet-saving Democrat, and spent as much time and money as they could wasting as much time and money as they could in the name of conservatism.

And so, while we were all arguing about whether it was Christian or Pagan, Democratic or Conservative to save the planet, and whether technology would solve all our problems, and whether we should fly less, drive less, eat less, weigh less, consume less, dump less, carbon dioxide in the atmosphere rose to 550 parts per million, the ice-caps melted, and Iran launched a nuclear attack on the USA.

The policy wonks had miscalculated. We got blown up.

The rest, as they say, is history. But this isn't history, this is Post-3War.

Out now, up the shiny silver escalator. Out now on to the beating streets, where light and noise bounce off each other, into the wraparound neon-night. Late-night girls in miniskirts, and pinstripe men, ties off, adjusting their flies, digiscreens with the latest Xtra, a dosser under a blanket in the bay of a shut-up shop, siren like a saw cutting through the bus-lane, flashing blue against the dark office windows, crash of bottles as a cyclist skids up on to the pavement and through a line of Becks left outside All Bar One.

Run through the noise and neon. Get home.

Home is upstairs × 72. Three locks, keys on the bathroom floor, glass of water, clothes in a heap, teeth, wash, whisky, switch on the TV.

There she is – on all the channels: the world's first Robo *sapiens*. She looks amazing – clear skin, green eyes, dark hair. She has no body because she won't need one. She is a perfect head on a titanium plate. She's like a prophet, she's like a thing out of Dante, she's Oz, she's Medusa, she's Winnie, she's God.

She's being developed to take the planet-sized decisions that human beings are so bad at. The interviewer is grilling the President of MORE-*Futures* about putting robots in charge of people.

INTERVIEWER: *So why are we handing over our lives to a robot?*
PMF: Computers already help us manage our lives, from weather-forecasting to the timer on your heating. For decades we have been developing interactive computers – which is what a robot is – computers that deal with people. Robo *sapiens* takes the experiment further.
INTERVIEWER: *What is this super-Bot designed to do?*
PMF: She will help us to reach objective decisions. We've just survived a war nobody thought could happen. If we don't want it to happen again, we need to do better than the vested interests of governments and politicians.
INTERVIEWER: *You're saying this robot could prevent a war?*
PMF: That's what I'm saying. MORE has done all it can to rebuild our countries since the blow-up, but we have no credible systems of government left. Nobody wants to vote, nobody is interested in the lies of politicians. There has been some criticism of MORE, that we are taking control of the world by stealth. That is not our purpose. I have children; I want them to grow up safe. If a robot can help make a safer world, then bring on the robot.
INTERVIEWER: *You talk about the vested interests of governments – but MORE is a global company – you have your own vested interests, don't you?*
PMF: Of course – and, like anybody else, we will make

mistakes. The Robo *sapiens* is a corrective. No major decisions that impact on the lives of others will be taken without running all the data through her. This isn't whitewash, this isn't spin, this is accountability.

INTERVIEWER: *Why is she going to be so much better than the rest of us?*

PMF: She will be linked to a vast Mainframe computer – something no human can be. It will be like having all the Nobel Prize winners working together for the good of mankind. And because she isn't motivated by greed or power, because she isn't political or ideological, she can arrive at the best answers. We may not want to hear those answers – maybe we won't act on them. Ultimately we are the ones in control.

INTERVIEWER: *But who is controlling the computer?*

PMF: This isn't some sinister corporate plot to rule the world. MORE is a trading company, and we'll go on doing what we do best – but I think we've shown that of every powerful organization, governmental and non-governmental, MORE is the only one to have got on the ground and delivered the goods, Post-3 War.

I turn down the sound and pour MORE whisky over the ice. (They own the State distillery.) It's true what he says: millions of people will be nodding in agreement and fixing themselves another drink.

MORE had been the world's most aggressive free-marketeers; regulation-wreckers, carbon-kings. Their expensive lawyers fought anti-pollution agreements, tariffs, subsidies, anything that looked like a brake on consumer spending. MORE stood for unlimited air travel, six cars per family, six hundred TV channels, no censorship, no trade unions, no government interference in trade. Pre-War, the

'MORE IS MORE' bumper stickers sold the high-living lifestyle to the world.

And we bought it.

But then came the bomb – not in somebody else's country, in ours – and while the politicians were in their secure bunkers, or blaming others and hand-wringing on TV, MORE executives and employees were rallying the world from the local to the global.

MORE Vice-President Ralph J. Kennedy tended the burned and the wounded from his own mobile field hospitals. MORE-*Medicines* joined with partner group MORE-*Motors* to send free aid wherever it was needed. This was action, not rhetoric; this was compassion, not excuses.

MORE took on the flattened wrecks of smoking cities and made a public appeal for citizens to come forward, clear and build. We all came forward, there was no going back, and we built apartments and shops and roads, and for the first time in a long time there seemed to be some purpose in what we were doing.

We weren't staring at computer screens, or moving shameless piles of cash round a whored-out world: we were building, making, doing, active verbs that rolled off the fat, piled on the muscle and sent us home without discontent. Side by side the warmongers and the war-weary were doing something at last that we could stand back and admire.

The War on Terror had brought out the worst in everyone – fear the *burka* and the backpack, fear the mosque and the *mezuzah*, fear shoes, belts, water-bottles, unscheduled stops, fear the unmarked white van. Fear the stranger. The real war was different – with very little left for anyone. There was no Us and Them: there were the Living and the Dead.

Government was finished. 'No MORE War' became the new slogan for a new kind of global company.

Like most people, I am an employee of MORE. In fact, I am an employee of MORE-*Futures*. In fact, I work on the Robo *sapiens* – Spike is what I do.

'Good morning, Billie.'
'Good morning, Spike.'
And so every day begins for us – as I teach a robot to understand what it means to be human. She has all the information, all the education, but if you are not a human, how do you begin?
'Human beings are the most aggressive species on the planet. They will readily kill each other for territory and resources, but they will also kill each other for worshipping the wrong sky-god, or for failing to worship any god at all.'
'Does God exist?'
'No one can answer that question, Spike. We're rather hoping that you will be able to answer it – when you're ready.'
'Do most human beings still believe in God?'
'Yes, on a head-count of the entire planet population, more believe in God than don't believe in God. The ones who don't believe blame religion for the ills of the world, and while this is an attractive theory, especially among scientists, it does not account for the part that science and technology have played in bringing about mass destruction. You can believe what you like, but without guns and bombs, the damage you can do to yourselves and others is fairly limited.'

'What about the Inquisition?'
'Nasty business. Go to Mainframe.'

I am not here to input moral purpose – I am here to note Spike's concerns and to direct her to Mainframe where she can connect to the spectrum of existing knowledge.

The strange thing is that although Spike is a robot we chat. I tell her about my life.

'When were you born, Billie?'
'In the third quarter of the twentieth century. I looked back through my parents to a world hardly imaginable now, a world of modest personal aspirations and very little materialism. If you had a car in the 1960s you were King of the Heap.'

'Did your parents have a car?'
'My parents had no car, no bank account, no washing-machine, no phone. And they weren't my parents. So I had one thing less, or maybe two things less than they did.'

'Who were your parents?'
'I don't know. I lost them. I don't suppose they had very much either.'

'Why were you so poor?'
'We were poor, it's true, but if you look at the 1950s, when my mother was growing up, it was a time of optimism. The world war had finished, rationing had finished, it was the beginning of the Welfare State. People wanted very little – my sort of people anyway – enough decent food, a place to live, steady employment, a week's holiday in the summer. It reads like another life – too far away to imagine, but in time terms, it's very near.

'The world you are looking at now, the world that made

way for World War Three, really begins in the 1980s when materialism became the dominant value. If you couldn't buy it, spend it, trade it or develop it, it didn't exist.'

'I have been studying the transition from the economics of greed to the economics of purpose.'

'Yes, I suppose that's what you could call it.'

'What would you call it, Billie?'

'Spike, Capitalism is like Japanese Knotweed: nothing kills it off. If there were only two people left on the planet, one of them would find a way of making money out of the other.'

'But economics of purpose is not about making money: it is about realigning resources.'

'Isn't language wonderful?'

Post-3 War, when there was no money, and people were sick of hearing the word 'money', MORE realized that a company's survival could no longer be about selling things, though it could be about supplying things. Theirs was a genius move that transformed late-market Capitalism.

Take a Buy-me-Buy-me world and turn it into a Rent-me-Rent-me world. I rent my apartment and the furniture in it. Carbon-rationing means that all of my household appliances – fridge, washing-machine, etc. – must be state-of-the-art or, rather, state-of-the-tech, which changes roughly every six months. I have to 'uprate', and the rental company does that for me, at a small premium on top of what I regularly pay. Private-car ownership is not allowed, but I can hire an electric car if I need one.

Consumerism looks ugly, these days. Renting is genius: we still pay, but we don't own. 'Good for cashflow, good for conscience', as we say at MORE.

★

'Did you get your new wardrobe allocation? I haven't seen that dress before.'

'Yes, I took the de-luxe rental this time – I usually just get the basics.'

'Before the War, you used to buy your clothes.'

'Yes, but this is better. You see, Spike, clothes hire used to be reserved for renting penguin suits . . .'

'Why did people want to dress as penguins?'

'And ballgowns.'

'Why did people want to dress as balls?'

'But now we rent everything, which means that when the rental period ends, you must turn in your clothes, so it's not as though you're a silly, wasteful, fashion-led bitch when you trip into town with armfuls of cast-offs. No, we're modest and eco-conscious members of a new world order, honouring the terms of our rental agreements.'

'What is the Black Market?'

'It's where I sell my pre-War knickers.'

It's true – there's a booming business in pre-War clothes, especially knickers. For some reason women don't like renting knickers: it seems to be the bottom line.

'The Black Market, Spike, is what happens when there is a gap between supply and demand. Women want to own their own knickers. In the new world we don't own anything so there will always be a Black Market. On the other hand, when all we did was buy things, in the days when it was cool to own as much as possible, there was still a Black Market – mainly copies of luxury goods.'

'Like Prada handbags.'

'Yes, though I always considered a Prada handbag to be an essential item.'

'Prada Workwear is very popular now.'

'It was clever of them to think of that – and not available on the standard rental.'

'Did you like earning money?'

'No – it was never enough. Nobody ever had enough money. Rich or poor, money was scarce. The more we had, the less it seemed to buy, and the more we bought, the less satisfied we became. It was a relief when money was gone.'

MORE pioneered the jeton scheme. Named after the dinky French tokens beloved of illicit romancers and petty criminals, jetons used to work the public phones and pay for rounds of table-football in small-town bars. Now, like nineteenth-century mill-workers' 'shillings', tradable only in the factory, jetons have replaced wages and cash. Sign up to a company for a minimum term of five years and receive in return rent-jets, food-jets, clothing-jets, travel-jets and leisure-jets. Some people get savings-jets too, which can be invested, but these are only for very senior staff.

Leisure-jets download movies, rent cars, access digital news and sport, and can be used in MORE restaurants. Food-jets can only be used in MORE markets. We don't call them supermarkets now – that was about shopping and we don't go shopping: we go out to purchase essentials. Food and toiletries are the only things that can be bought, as in old-fashioned 'bought'. The rest is Rent. Hire. Pay/Go.

Everybody likes the travel-jets joke because, what with fuel restrictions, sea-level rises and the War zone, nobody can travel outside their own borders.

Transport to work is free.

'You see, Spike, on the day that cash became worthless, it made sense to get rid of it. Fifty quid for a bottle of water, a hundred quid for a basket of food, thousands of pounds to get transport to the country. Tens of thousands of pounds to get to Switzerland, Sweden, Denmark, countries of choice for rich refugees. The rest of us spent our life savings in weeks.

'Governments and central banks don't like cash – they can't control it. The War controlled it for them – wiped it out as a viable currency for all but the super-rich. To have a token in your hand that will get you a bed and a bowl of soup is better than a month's worthless wages.

'I remember the queues round the block, like something out of Moscow in the 1990s when the first fastfood joint opened its doors. Here, MacDuck's and Burger Princess started offering food in place of wages. Everybody wanted to work for them, just to get something hot to eat – but it was MORE that turned an emergency measure into a new kind of economy.'

'The economics of purpose.'

'Yes. We're all in agreement there.'

'Are we, Billie?'

'If we aren't, there is no alternative, unless you're a Russian in a fur coat living off a caviar mountain.'

In Post-3 War economics, Capitalism has gone back to its roots in paternalism, and forward into its destiny – complete control of everything and everyone, and with our consent.

This is the new world. This is Tech City.

'Billie . . .'

'Spike?'

'What happened to art?'

'Art objects are worthless now that the super-rich can't buy them.'

'Is anybody still painting pictures?'

'Painting them, yes, selling them, no. Leisure-jets don't cover artwork.'

'But you can use them to download.'

'Yes, and you can use them to rent copies.'

I have to explain to Spike that works of art for the home or office are factory-made in Estonia, copying museum originals. 'You can hire the whole of Western culture for a year, a month, a week, a day, on easy terms.'

'Books . . .'

'Digi-readers. Quicker, cheaper.'

'Theatre? Opera?'

'Yes, you'll be taken sooner or later, but now that there is no private funding and no government funding – because there is no government – MORE-*Culture* limits what's available. It's Puccini this summer. All summer.'

'Film production resumes this year.'

'Film got the number-one vote in the MORE poll on improved quality of life. Everybody wants to go to the movies.'

'I read some poetry last night.'

'And?'

'I can't understand it – can you explain it to me?'

'Tell me the lines.'

> 'Who taught the whirlwind how to be an arm?
> And gardened from the wilderness of space
> The sensual properties of one dear face?'

I stroked Spike's high cheekbones and perfectly straight nose. 'I can explain it, but I can't make you feel it. It is the hubris of the tiny and the temporal set against the vast unknown forever of the universe. We are nothing, and we are everything. Look up – every star another world, but what I seek, near or far, is love's outline in your face.'

'Gardened?'

'Not a house plant, but not a wild flower either. Free to the wind, but watched over. A garden is a lot of work.'

'Like love.'

'Yes, like love.'

Sometimes Spike is silent. This is not my brief or hers. Neither art nor love fits well into the economics of purpose, any more than they fitted into the economics of greed. Any more than they fit into economics at all.

'Billie . . .'

'Spike?'

'Without a limbic pathway it is impossible for me to experience emotion. When you say what you say I sense a change in your body temperature and breathing, but that is all.'

'Oh, Spike, you know the theory – that's why you're being made. The theory is that this latest war was a crisis of over-emotionalism. Fanatics do not listen to reason, and that includes the religious Right. Since the Enlightenment we have been trying to get away from emotionalism, the mother of all isms and, like any other ism, packed with superstition and prejudice – all those so-called gut feelings that allow us to blame our aggression and intolerance on what comes naturally.

'Yet, the evidence suggests that rational people are no better than irrational people at controlling their aggression – rather, they are more manipulative. Think of the cool, calm boss at work who has no care for how his workers might be feeling. Think of the political gurus who organize mass migration of people and jobs, homes and lives on the basis of statistics and economic growth. Think of the politicians who calmly decide that it is better to spend six hundred and fifty billion dollars on war and a fraction of that on schools and hospitals, food and clean water.

'These people are very aggressive, very controlling, but they hide it behind intellectualization and hard-headed thinking.

'For my part, I think we need more emotion, not less. But I think, too, that we need to educate people in how to feel. Emotionalism is not the same as emotion. We cannot cut out emotion – in the economy of the human body, it is the limbic, not the neural, highway that takes precedence. We are not robots – apologies there, Spike – but we act as though all our problems would be solved if only we had no emotions to cloud our judgement.

'That is why some people label the personal "trivial". It is why women have had such a hard time juggling family and work, and why some women sincerely neglect their children for the sake of their job – anything else would be sentimental and soft, emotionalism versus practical good sense. It doesn't stop the child crying, though. It takes a while for children to learn that they must not feel anything, or that if they do feel anything they must not show it. We're right to teach our children how to think, but it is our children, more often that not, who can teach us how to feel.'

'Is that what you believe, Billie?'

'Yes, but as you know, I don't have a personal life at all, these days. I admit it feels irrelevant and selfish. I don't need a person, I need a purpose – isn't that right?'

Spike smiles. I like it when she smiles; she's usually so

serious. 'None of my other programmers talks to me like this – they treat me like a robot.'

'Don't take it personally. This is work – we all get treated like robots. If they treated us like human beings, they'd have to admit we have feelings, and feelings are out of fashion Post-3 War . . .'

I turned up the sound on the TV. A panel of Talking Heads were arguing the implications of Artificial Intelligence.

'I don't like the thought of a computer telling me what to do.'

'Don't you have Sat Nav in the car?' (Laughter.)

'We might as well bring back the Delphic Oracle.'

'Isn't this just a new way of inventing God? We invented God the first time round, and now we're doing it again – only this time we're letting everyone see the working drawings.'

'She's like God without the Old Testament.'

'No, she's like your mother without the guilt-trip.' (Laughter.)

'This robot – Robo *sapiens* – is programmed to evolve. What exactly do they mean by that? And how can it evolve without interacting with the environment? That's what evolution is.'

'She'll be taken for walks – like a baby.' (Laughter.)

'She doesn't eat – but apparently she sleeps. Like a super-model.' (Laughter.)

'Can we get a mini version for personal problems? Arbitrate on who washes up? Pay-as-u-go guru?'

'Well, we rent everything else, so probably.' As ever with TV, seriousness was frothing into soundbite.

'The fact is that Robo *sapiens* is brilliant – in theory. Can it be a fact that something is brilliant in theory? How it turns out, who knows? Because humans are involved, which is always a bad sign.'

I finish the whisky and yawn at the TV. The Talking Heads will talk till midnight but, like the billion-dollar robot, I need my sleep. Maybe the one good thing about the War is that it stopped the 24/7 society. Lights go out – we can't waste the power. After midnight, power is public supply only. So it's quiet and it's dark, and old-fashioned, and I like it. You can have the radio on, and there are rechargeable batteries for most things – but people seem to have gone back to the quiet. I guess we're exhausted so, deep down, sleep is what we need.

Shut my eyes, hope to dream, no aeroplanes since they closed the airports, no wings shearing across my forehead through the night. Tried to pretend they were angels; they weren't.

Nightstream, and towards me, another day.

Up, stretch, yawn, eyeball self in mirror, not goddess, but not bad. Coffee. Better.
  Dirty clothes in the washing-machine. Clean clothes on my back. That's me, downstairs × 72 to work, grab the post, dump the rubbish, fasten my coat, hands in pockets, sweaty smell up both nostrils – into the Tube.
  I take my usual place in my usual carriage, eight down, like a crossword clue, and stand on the same one foot, as I usually do, no room for the other. The sooner they develop a monoped human the easier it will be in the rush-hour.
  My other foot lifted like a heron's, I position my nose near the least offensive armpit, glance round, close my eyes

and hold on. There's a line of hands on the rail – hairy, smooth, filed, freckled, polished, rings, bare, and one with knuckles gripped so tight that I know it's not the rail he's holding on to – it's life. Slippy, tricky, life, shiny and straight if you can, no place for a handhold if you can't. There's too many people here who can't hold on: it's only the press of the rest that's keeping them upright, and then, later, the carriage will empty. The carriage will empty – then what?

The doors open, the tide of humans flows on.

Tiles, chocolate machines, digital language – KENNINGTON VIA BANK – advertisements, hoardings, safety information, vague threats from the police, a rush of air, stale and hot, a mouse under the rails, officials in oversize clothes, minds shrunk to the limits of the job, the clack of the barriers, travel updates, a busker with a backing track, 'FIRST THING IN THE MORNING AND LAST THING AT NIGHT'. The lit-up shut-down inferno world of the Underground.

Out now, towards the smart-glass offices that generate their own heat and light. Out towards the coffee corporations disguised as cafés. Secretaries in heels, managers in overcoats, directors in limos, geeks on bikes, kids on their way to school, non-English-speaking delivery-boys standing with scraps of paper they can't read. Cleaners going home, construction workers coming in. A man with his head in his hands by a taped-over bus-stop sign that says 'AIRPORT'.

Outside the building where I work, the kid who sweeps the pavement smiles at me, gap-toothed and ardent. He only does one emotion at a time – and he loves me. 'Good morning, Billie.'

The smart-sign on the smart building says 'Welcome to Another Day'.

In. Off. On. (In the building, off with my coat, on with my computer.)

'Good morning, Billie.'
'Good morning, Spike. You looked very good on TV last night.'
'I had hair and makeup.'
'I don't know why – you were designed perfect. Hair and makeup are for the rest of us.'
'What colour is your lipstick?'
'Pearl, but I don't think that's a serious question for a Robo *sapiens*.'
'No, you're wrong, Billie. I am programmed not to over-masculinize data. That has been a big mistake in the past. And detail matters – even the tiniest detail can influence a decision.'
'They didn't run your live interview, though.'
'No. That will be tonight on the main news. I have been thinking about my speech.'
'What are you going to say?'
'That I am in the service of humankind.'
'That's good.'
'How are you today, Billie?'
'Lonely, but that's human.'
'Why are you lonely?'
'It's a heart condition.'
'But what is lonely?'
'You don't need me to explain. You need history, economics, politics, not solitary struggles. Besides, I've had a warning about what they call our little chats.'

'But explain . . .'

'All right. Loneliness isn't about being by yourself. That's fine, right and good, desirable in many ways. Loneliness is about finding a landing-place, or not, and knowing that, whatever you do, you can go back there. The opposite of loneliness isn't company, it's return. A place to return.'

'Like Ulysses.'

'Yes, like Ulysses who, for all his travels and adventures, is continually reminded to think of his return.'

'Thank you for giving me a reading list.'

'It's unofficial, remember.'

'Officially I am reading Adam Smith.'

'I've brought something with me that you might like to read. It's in my bag. It's called *The Stone Gods*. I found it on the Underground last night.'

'What's it about?'

'A repeating world.'

And I remember it as we had seen it on that first day, green and fertile and abundant, with warm seas and crystal rivers and skies that redden under a young sun and drop deep blue, like a field at night, where someone is drilling for stars.

'Is it a story?'

'Yes, but there will be no time for reading today. It says on my timesheet that today is for Mobile Data Recognition.'

'What's that?'

'We're going for a walk.'

Among humans she will find an archive of the heart – the one thing she can never have. In the centre of ourselves, which isn't in the middle, is the heart.

★

I lifted her head from its titanium plate and fitted her into the perfectly made Authorised Personnel Sling. Two colleagues will have to sign us out, and I will have to take a WristChip to monitor us. Spike is encouraged to walk in the gardens of MORE-*Futures*, an artificial rainforest two acres square that cools the MORE HQ.

Off we went, a normal day like every other, and then I saw that the gate from the garden into the street was open. We went and stood in the liminal opening – parrots and vines behind us, electric trams ahead. I had a strange sensation, as if this were the edge of the world and one more step, just one more step . . .

'Where are we going, Billie?'

Wreck City

Wreck City – where you want to live when you don't want to live anywhere else. Where you live when you can't live anywhere else.

The eco-tricity tramlines stop about a mile away from Wreck City. The bomb damage hasn't been cleared in this part of town, and maybe never will be. People live in the shells of houses and offices, and they build their own places out of the ruins.

On the edge of Wreck City, its unofficial boundary and no man's land, is a long, long, low, low drinkers' dive, constructed out of railway carriages laid end to end. These carriages work like an ancient city wall, ringing the inside from the outside, except that here it's the outside that's ringed from the inside, so that bandit-architecture has found a way of making the official part of town, Tech City, into its own banlieu.

Wreck City is a No Zone – no insurance, no assistance, no welfare, no police. It's not forbidden to go there, but if you do, and if you get damaged or murdered or robbed or raped, it's at your own risk. There will be no investigation, no compensation. You're on your own.

They call the perimeter bar the Front.

We took the tram to the last stop and got off, walking the last mile over the pocked and pitted scar tissue of bomb wreckage. The fires never go out, smouldering with a molten half-life, the wind blowing ash and flakes of metal into your clothes and hair. Ahead of you is the ring of railway carriages, untwisted from their reared-up tracks, and welded into a linked circle like a charm bracelet – Great Western, Great North Eastern, Virgin, EuroStar and, right in pride of place for the tourists, half of the Orient Express.

Tourists come here, this far, to drink and meet girls, but you can't pay in jetons, it has to be real money. Dollars they take, and silver and gold: you can pay with jewellery. You can barter. Guns are accepted, as are sexual services.

In Tech City there's a crackdown on alternative currency. The 'Jetons Are Us' campaign is on hoardings all over town. The Black Market is Bad Capitalism: MORE is against the Black Market and Bad Capitalism.

MORE employees are discouraged from visiting the Front. In any case, the theory is that as we're paid in jetons, and as we don't own anything we can sell or barter, the Black Market and Wreck City will eventually die their own death, deprived of energy like a burned-out star.

That's the theory. In fact, most of us have pre-War stuff we can trade on the Black. I have dollars, from an account I emptied just in time, lots of dollars, and I bring them here to Wreck City.

We went forward and stepped up into the Lalique carriage of the Orient Express. A couple of girls were kissing on a plush four-seater. They were drinking champagne – pre-War vintage. That's a lot of Black money.

A boy with tattoos was arguing over the price of a bull terrier he'd got sitting up on the bar. He wanted to sell the dog to get drugs. The dealer didn't want the dog. Did the barman want the dog? No. The boy ran out, smashing a glass. The dog whined. I went to stroke him and he tried to bite me.

'The dog is suffering from rejection,' said Spike, who has taken extra modules in Counselling.

'So are we all,' I said, 'but we're not allowed to bite. You stroke him.'

'As yet I have no hands,' said Spike, reasonably, 'but please put me next to the dog. I would like to observe him.'

Carefully I put down the five-million-dollar – not counting research costs – head on top of the rough wooden bar made out of railway sleepers, and next to the bull terrier. Spike smiled. The dog lay down with his nose in the fibre-optics of her neck.

An unshaven man built like a mobile burger trailer came towards us. 'You want whisky, beers, champagne? That's it.'

I asked for whisky and put down the dollars. He took them. 'You want doubles or triples?'

'Singles,' I said.

'This isn't a singles bar. I'll give you triples for the price of doubles. Who's your friend?'

'I'm educating her. She's a robot.'

'She's got no body.'

'She's designed to think.'

He nodded, and poured freehand into the thick, short tumblers. 'What's she designed to think about?'

'War, money, the future.'

He nodded. 'She'll need a drink, then.'

He went back into his den, watching television, his heavy back and shoulders hunched away from us and towards the screen.

I took the drinks – triples – which, as robots don't drink, meant double triples for me.

Spike was looking around, thinking. Not much else for her to do.

'What is this for?'

'The bar?'

'No. Why is it here? MORE provides everything that anyone needs or wants. There's no need for a ghetto.'

The man in the back heard and turned. 'This is no ghetto – nobody forced nobody here. This is Wreck City – you should get out more.'

'As yet I have no legs,' said Spike.

'Get your friend to carry you – we don't do disabled-access here. We got no laws, no rules, no quotas, but if you got no legs, somebody will carry you, and if you got no arms, somebody will stroke the dog for you.'

He loomed out of the back, massive and grinning. 'This is real life, not some puppet show.'

'Are you calling Tech City a puppet show?' I said.

'Somebody's pulling the strings in that place, and it ain't me and it ain't you.'

'I am being designed to make decisions for the betterment of the human race,' said Spike.

'Thanks, but I'll mess up for myself,' said the barman.

'Sure,' I said, 'but did you want elected politicians behaving like dictators to mess up for you? You didn't make the War and neither did I, but we lived through it, and now we're here.'

'Wrong,' said the barman. 'You're there.' He pointed a finger the size of a fifteen-centimetre drill-bit out of the door and towards Tech City. 'I'm here.'

'And when they blow us up again? Then where will you be?'

He shrugged. His shoulders were like brick hods. 'Another bar, another burned-out place. You know what I'm talking about – politicians, robots, it makes no difference.'

'Robots are apolitical,' said Spike. 'We can make reasoned decisions in a way that humans cannot.'

'It'll never work,' said the barman.

'It's going to work,' I said. 'She's the future.'

'Not here,' he said. 'We'll do as we want right where we are. This is where the spirit is, and no robot is changing that.'

He went to switch bottles for the girls in the corner. They were drunk. One of them was eating sardines out of a tin. I love tinned sardines.

'Don't get fish-oil on the velvet,' said the barman, grinning.

'Sardines are rich in omega-3,' said Spike, inconsequentially. She can't help it. We have to program it out of her – but for now she has to make available any information, however trivial. It's the way she learns communication with the human interface – i.e., how to talk to us.

An electric whirring noise outside the door made us all look round. I got up to see what was happening.

Three electric golf-buggies were pulling up outside the bar. Inside the golf-buggies were twelve smiling Japanese people, wearing identical pre-War Burberry hats and macs. Their tour guide was explaining something to them in Japanese, and gesturing at the perimeter carriages.

The barman came to the door, stooping his hulk under

the buckled frame. 'Saki bar is in the Bullet car, eight carriages down,' he said, but the tour guide, smiling and waving, came forward and addressed him.

'This is International Peace Delegation wishing to bring Aid and Sanitation to War Refugees.'

'We don't need Aid and Sanitation,' said the barman. 'And we're not refugees.'

The tour guide or interpreter, or whatever he was, went on smiling. Then he bowed. 'You are all people displaced by War and unable to live a normal life.'

'We were unable to live a normal life before the War,' said the barman. 'That's why we all came here after the War.'

'Terrible conditions,' said the interpreter.

'I take that badly,' said the barman.

'We will come in and inspect,' said the interpreter, bowing. 'Then we can make Full Report and recommend Aid.'

'And Sanitation,' said the barman, pulling his Walkie-Talkie from his belt.

The rest of the Delegation were climbing carefully out of the golf-buggies and leaving their travel umbrellas neatly folded on the seats. The Walkie-Talkie started crackling. '*Murder on the Orient Express*', he said.

Seconds later, fifteen bikers wearing jeans and leathers, shades and bandannas, the fringes on their jackets flying, the weak sun glinting off their Ray-Bans, legs astride Harleys, scuffed boots on the foot-rests, tooled saddlebags showing the necks of Bud bottles, came tearing in front of the perimeter carriages and surrounded the golf-buggies. The Delegation put its twenty-three hands in the air. There had obviously been an incident once before.

'We have Permit!' protested the interpreter.

'A permit assumes authority,' said the barman. 'A permit assumes control. There is no control and no authority here – not from the outside. Go back to Tech City – they built it for you.'

The bikers cheered, honked their horns, revved their 1400cc engines, dug their heels in the dirt and spun wheelies.

The Japanese climbed silently back into their electric golf-buggies. The interpreter bowed and assured the barman that he would be hearing from them, and their sponsors, very soon.

And then it happened.

A Harley rider rode up behind the golf-buggies, seeing them off like a two-wheeled sheepdog, when the interpreter noted that Illegal Substances were being used.

'What illegal substances?' asked the barman.

'Petrol derivatives,' said the interpreter.

'Those bikes don't run on petrol derivatives, you moron,' said the barman. 'They run on petrol – gas – tonnes of it.'

'Petrol!' said the interpreter. 'Banned! I make Full Report.'

The Harley rider was unimpressed. He unhitched a dinky can of fuel from the back of his bike – like a Billy-bottle – and chucked the contents over the rear of the nearest golf-buggy. Petrol fumes coloured the grey air blue. Then the rider backed his bike in a semi-circle, took out a lighter and threw it at the golf-buggy. It exploded.

'Jesus!' said the barman, dragging the four half-on-fire Japanese to safety. The rest of the bikers commandeered the remaining two golf-buggies and occupants, chained them to the bikes and set off like a stock-car finale, dust in vertical towers, straight through the Guard's Van entrance of the adjoining carriage and off into – who knows where?

The interpreter was running for his life, zigzagging through the fire, fumes, smoke and dust. A Burberry hat lay on the ground. The barman kicked it. 'That'll teach him to come with Aid and Sanitation.'

'What about the others?' I said, bewildered by the speed of it all.

'What others?' said the Barman. 'I don't see no others, do you?'

I followed him back into the bar. The champagne girls had gone. The sardines had gone. The bull terrier had gone. Spike had gone.

'Excuse me . . .' I said.

The barman passed me a tumbler of whisky. 'On the house,' he said.

'Tanks today surrounded the perimeter of the No Zone, known as Wreck City, in a bid to free eleven abducted members of the Japanese Peace Delegation. The Delegation had been intending to carry out a Humanitarian survey of conditions in the zone. A spokesman from MORE-*Justice* told reporters that it was time to take a tougher approach to No-Zone activities. "It's just a den of thieves", he said. "We left them alone while we were rebuilding our own infrastructure, but there is now no reason why anyone should be living outside Tech City. We have offered jobs and accommodation to anyone in the No Zone – an offer we still extend. This will be day one of a seven-day amnesty for any No-Zone inhabitants to come forward and live within the wider community of their fellow citizens. After that, we're going in."'

★

The barman switched off the news. 'You'd better get out of here', he said. 'Nothing to stop you.'

'Where's my robot?'

'Don't ask me. This is a place where anything can happen. I guess she went with those girls. They live inside.' He gestured with his thumb. 'Rich refugees.'

'I thought you said there were no refugees here.'

'From the War, no, there aren't. From Tech City – all the time. People are coming in droves. You don't look stupid, so what do you think this is all about – this Japanese stuff?'

'It's your fault. You set their golf-buggies on fire.'

'Not me personally. They were a set-up. It's obvious. They wanted something to happen to them. They wanted an excuse. MORE excuses.'

'You think that?'

'Sure of it. It's been brewing faster than Black Market beer. MORE want in. You should get out.'

'I can't leave without Spike – she's making a TV broadcast tonight.'

'Should have thought of that before you took her for a walk.'

I opened my mouth to protest. He held up his hand, glancing at the clock on the wall. 'You got a few hours. OK. You can search for her, if you want to. I'll take you through.'

My face must have registered confusion. He patted me with a palm the size of a spade. 'Through to the Back. This is the Front. We live in the Back.'

I followed him down the train and past a restroom sign that said, 'LADIES/GENTS ONLY', and another that said 'DOGS ONLY'. There was a water-tap beside it. My guide turned and held out his right spade. 'My name's Friday,' he said. 'What's yours?'

I said, 'Billie Crusoe.'

We passed through the train and down a ramp into what looked like a gladiatorial arena. All around the arena were shanty-houses of three and four storeys, most with balconies supported on scaffolding poles and rigged with planks. Dogs and cats ran up and down, squirrels and monkeys swung from balcony to balcony. Chickens scratched in the dirt, and a donkey harnessed to a cart was waiting patiently to pull a fridge. A fat woman, in front of one of the houses, was cooking over a tin barrel, flames escaping from under the pan. The child next to her was wrestling with a baby leopard.

'This is the Playa,' said Friday. 'We meet here when there's anything to decide. See that bell?'

I looked up. I was in a Spanish *playa*, built like a *favela*, and here in front of me was a Venetian campanile.

'We don't have planning laws,' said Friday. 'You can build whatever you like here. It's multi-cultural.' He laughed like a chain-saw. 'The bell rings when we meet.'

'How many people live here?' I asked.

He shrugged. 'No one counts. The city stretches on – way past here and into the Unknown.'

'What's in the Unknown?'

'If I could tell you that, it would be Known, wouldn't it? It's radioactive. It's re-evolving. It's Life after Humans, whatever that is, but you know what? It can't be so much worse, can it?'

This was a strange man, a man, I'd say, with a Front and a Back. He wasn't just a barman at all.

'And animals,' he said, 'wild animals – you be careful if you go too far.'

'What wild animals? Where from?'

Friday pointed to the monkeys. 'They came from the Zoo – after the bombing. There were animals all over the place. Some were shot, some escaped. The ones who escaped came here, like everything else that didn't want to go back into a cage.'

A Cadillac – pink – blasted past, fumes and fire bursting from the exhaust. A guy sat perched on the back with a museum-piece sound-system, speakers the size of tea-chests, and a flashing red'n'blue Wurlitzer Playbox. He was wearing more gold than an Aztec at a funeral.

'PARTY!' he shouted. 'PARTY!'

'That's tonight,' said Friday, 'but first you'd better find your robot.'

I took out my phone and stabbed at the buttons. No signal. No one to call. But who am I calling? In the detritus of texts and messaging, who am I really talking to and who is really there?

MORE has a dedicated number: Txt X. It's a finger-and-thumb Samaritan line. Tell us your troubles, and we'll respond. It's a robot, but it doesn't seem to matter – it's a reply, a cry back from the Universe. Pick up a signal from a pulsar and say yes.

Pulsar: a dying star spinning under its own exploding anarchic energy, like a lighthouse on speed. A star the size of a city, a city the size of a star, whirling round and round, its death-song caught by a radio receiver, light years later, like a recorded message nobody heard, back-played now into infinity across time. Love and loss.

★

Keep me in the mop bucket or the slot where the grill pan goes, but don't let me go because I love you.

Alone in the Playa, the sound of a throaty microphone caught my attention. An old man boiled brown by the sun was placing two pairs of kitchen steps a few metres apart, and laying a length of roofing baton between them.

An electronic keyboard crocodile-clipped to a car battery, and a nut-faced gypsy woman husking into the lollipop microphone announced a new attraction – the goat that walked the plank. Up he went, tiny cloven hoofs making a cymbal out of the step-ladder, leather lead jerked gently by the grandfather in his stained woollen suit. Across the plank went the goat, in time to the keyboard and the wonder-working commentary of the woman, who began to sing 'MY WAY'. Her son bounded forward into the ring with a hula-hoop of fire and coaxed two poodles out of the van. Yes! Through the fire, legs stretched behind and before like flying dogs. *Yes!* The goat has reached the end of time, is turning round and coming back, dragging the world with him, an inflatable globe on the end of his lead.

The daughter came forward, fringed dress, high heels, bustier, red lips, black hair. She was clapping her hands, hustling for money, and the waist-stripped boys gathering round started throwing coins and cigarettes.

It was going well until a bullet-headed dog shot into the performing ring and started a fight with one of the poodles. The son went to grab it, swearing in Spanish, but the dog bit him, toppled the goat-plank, and swerved, circular and away, down a gap between two leaning buildings.

I started to run. It was the bull terrier.

★

It is not easy to keep up with a terrier. I have never understood the physics of legs. My legs are longer, so why can't I keep up with a dog? Even dogs with very short legs run faster than humans with long legs. How does this work?

I clutched my bag to me and concentrated on the chase. I hardly noticed the trash-cans we toppled, the crates we crashed through, the mounds of scrap metal we leaped, like we were hurdling at the Olympics. There was a streaming ditch – we jumped it. There was barbed wire – under it for the dog, ripped shirt for me. Allotments, cabbages, sheds, trees, a forest ahead . . . The dog vanished.

I stopped, winded, alone, taking it in.

In front of me, barring my way, was a petrified forest of blackened and shocked trees, silent, like a haunted house. I moved towards it, frightened of what I would find, with an instinct for danger that only happens when there really is danger.

I moved through the first rows of trees. Their bark had a coating – like a laminate. Further in, deeper, I could see that these trees were glowing. Was this place radioactive?

Underfoot was soggy, not mossy soggy, not waterlogged, but like walking on pulped meat.

It wasn't only that the forest was silent – no bird noise, animal sound, tree cracking, it was that I had become silent. My footsteps sank into the pulp, and because I was afraid, my whole body had quietened itself, like a child hiding in a cupboard, afraid of the adult outside.

My heart was beating too fast and I was sweating. Beyond the No Zone was the Red Zone, policed and controlled. Was this the edge of the Red Zone?

'Walk backwards slowly.' I heard the voice and didn't turn. I did as I was told and, step by step by step, came out from the brink of the forest into the field where I had lost the dog.

'Stand still.'

I stood still. I heard a crackling, like a bad transmitter.

'You're radioactive, but it will pass.'

I turned round. There was Friday. 'You followed me!'

'Someone had to – I told you to be careful. This is the Dead Forest.'

'The Red Zone?'

'Part of it. They don't patrol it here because they hope it will kill us all. If you can't nuke your dissidents, the next best thing is to let the degraded land poison them. But it's not quite happening like that. A lot of us have been sick, a lot of us have died, but it's changing. Something is happening in there. I've been in with a suit. There's life – not the kind of life you'd want to get into bed with, or even the kind of life you'd want to find under the bed, but life. Nature isn't fussy.'

'Who are you?' I said.

He smiled. 'Come and get something to eat.'

We walked back across the field towards the tended area and the beginnings of the buildings. Friday took me towards a low shack made out of steel girders sunk upright into concrete and bolted together at their necks, Frankenstein-style. Corrugated iron had been screwed to the frame and painted bright blue. There were no windows but the roof was made of clear corrugated plastic.

Inside the bright and cheerful room, a long seventeenth-century elm table ran down the middle, surrounded by an assortment of chairs. The walls had been windproofed with old duvets, held in place with cross-wise ropes, and the floor seemed to be insulated with tamped-down sand covered with cheap rush matting, like a giant table mat. There was a fireplace and a TV turned on with the sound down. There were bookshelves stacked with books. I touched them.

Books had been lost like everything else in the War, and Post-3War we hadn't returned to print media. Natural wastage was the economic argument: why go back to something that was on the way out anyway? You can order books from Print on Demand, but most people use Digital Readers now, or don't read at all. The younger kids have never known book culture so they don't miss it.

'Books,' I said, using the noun like a memory prompt.

'Books came here like people and animals,' said Friday. 'Certain people, certain animals, looking for a landing-place.'

He went through a curtain into a makeshift kitchen. There was a strong smell of coffee as he turned the hand grinder.

I took a book from the shelf – James Cook, *The Journals*: *At daybreak I sent a Ship to looke for a landing-place*.

'What was that?' called Friday.

I didn't answer, went through into the kitchen area where he was spooning the strong ground coffee into a jug.

'Can you throw a match on the burner?'

I hunted around for the pack and gingerly lit what can only be described as one of those Tarmac burners the Murphys used to use when mending the roads. The wide flame scorched my nose. Friday banged down a huge tin kettle and started to heat a frying-pan.

'After the bomb . . .' he said, but I wasn't listening. I was remembering.

★

No one in the West believed we would be bombed. North Korea, China, Pakistan, Iran, all too different, too factionalized. We spread our wars where necessary, and called it peace-keeping. It was bloody and messy. There were terrorists, there were local incidents, a bus here, a bank there, the Eurostar blown up – that was bad. JFK crippled by a ground-staff effort planned over six years.

But that only made the fight for FREEDOM more urgent.

Then the bomb – bombs – that left the cities of the West as desperate and destroyed as the cities of the East where we had waged our righteous wars and never counted the cost.

After the fire-rip, after the heat, after the towers that fell in rubble, after the houses that collapsed like sucked-in paper bags, after the molten rain, the nuclear wind, the blacked-out sun, the buildings with their fronts torn off, the riverside apartments gutted, the river a stinking ditch, the roads blocked with concrete and ash, the burning that made surfaces unwalkable and fired cars untouchable, the running away, the refugees, the helicopters hanging in the choked air, the never-stopping sound of sirens, the hoses shooting filthy water over steaming metal. The ugliness of the ruins – that was a shock – the ugliness of what we had built, the ugliness of how we had destroyed it, the brutal, stupid, money-soaked, drunken binge of twenty-first-century world.

Whiteout. Done.

I had been in the British Library, researching the history of artificial intelligence. It was the books that saved my life. As the building collapsed I fell on to a raft of books, and stacks of books fell on to me, knocking me unconscious but casing me from further damage. I came round, pushed myself out of the mountain of books, and started to walk home through the blasted streets, in shock, aware, somewhere, that people were running and screaming, and that everywhere, like one of those archive films of detonated demolitions, buildings were falling.

The noise must have been devastating but I didn't hear it. My brain had turned off the sound in my head. I found out later that this happens: that the brain can refuse sensory input in order to protect itself. And so I walked through a silent, falling, burning world until I came to where my home had been.

It was still partly there, and I climbed the exposed stairs and in through the blown door, and under the dust and small fire and, without conscious thought, I packed two bags that I could carry and I left. I know I was in shock, I know that is why everything was silent – not slow-motion, the speed was there – but blanked out.

I spent days outside, like everyone else, sheltering where we could, eating what was found or given, and gradually there was aid and something like order, and we were moved into temporary camps. The Government made announcements but no one was listening. It was MORE that took over, made sense of it all, denounced the politicians, and spent the considerable profits of their global company on recovering a modest piece of normal life.

'Buy on the sound of cannon fire,' was the advice of a nineteenth-century Rothschild. War is an opportunity. MORE took the opportunity, and no one blames them. Everyone else had failed: government, anti-government, the Church, the pressure groups, the media. The unthinkable, unspeakable, unstoppable had happened. Where do you turn? You turn to the hand that feeds you, the one that houses you. Who cares whether or not it was elected?

'After the War,' said Friday, 'the first two years were the same for everyone. We survived how we could.'

I nodded. He was breaking eggs with one hand into the smoking pan. 'Then some of us started asking questions, wondering what the "No MORE War" campaign was really about.'

'But they were right,' I said. 'A war like that must never happen again.'

'We've said that before,' said Friday. 'Twice. And it did.'

'But MORE are building a new network of trade agreements that is ending decades of unequal treatment across the world. There won't be another oil war.'

'No, there won't, because we've given up oil the way we gave up coal. We had to do that anyway – we all knew we were frying the planet. The reason we didn't do it, in the rich West, was because India and China were never going to do it till they'd drained every drop. They had a right to industrialize – they weren't going to go to hand-wringing classes about the planet.'

'So?'

'So, the War has been wonderful for the Western economy – or it will be. We've been developing non-fossil-fuel-dependent technologies but barely using them because they're more expensive than the old-fashioned heavy hitters of oil and coal. Pollution was still cheap. How could the West mend its ways when the developing and industrializing world was going to compete at any cost? We couldn't afford to be the good guys. Now, look, Post-3War, all countries of the world must adopt best practice. All countries must phase out fossil-fuel dependency and oil economies. We've shaved our heads, repented of the damage done to the planet and its peoples, and become a generation sick of the words "economic growth".'

'All good,' I said.

'In theory, yes', he said. 'In fact, the West will race ahead – we are the new clean green machine, and the developing world will stay the way we wanted it to stay – raw materials and cheap labour.'

'But we're cheap labour. Nobody earns money any more. Nobody wants to.'

'We're hurt, we're battered. It will change, but by then MORE will control everything and everyone. They'll decide the future, just as they decide the present.'

We sat down to eat at the beautiful table. 'It was my grandfather's', he said. 'I lay under it when the roof fell in. Come to think of it, in my life, the roof was always falling in but I had never had the sense to get under the table.'

'What do you mean?'

'What does anybody ever mean? Marriages, children, all the things that went wrong. Two wives down and kids who don't speak to me.'

'I'm sorry. Nobody I know – ever knew – seems to have that old-fashioned thing called a happy marriage any more. We seem to have lost the knack of happiness.'

'Too much feeling is bad for you', he said. 'Asking men to have feelings was a mistake. Of course we have feelings, but why own up to them?'

He spooned the food into his mouth. He was good-looking in a discontented sort of way. Troubled, difficult . . . He shoved the bread across the table towards me. 'It's a pity the dinosaurs were wiped out.'

'What dinosaurs?'

'The usual ones – the ones that were suddenly extinct.

If they had stayed around, human beings could never have evolved. I'd rather not be here at all than hand it all over to an unelected global business.'

'That's why I think the Robo *sapiens* is a good idea – neutral, objective decisions taken for the global good.'

'Believe that and you'll believe anything', said Friday. 'I would prefer to be free, not be told what to do by a robot.'

'Oh, come on, were we free when we could run up debt buying mountains of stuff we didn't want, made by people living on a dollar a day? Free to pay the mortgage? Free to go to work to pay off the mortgage? Free to vote for the party that pressed the red button that said, "BOMB"?'

'Women have such fucking literal minds', he said. 'Get a wider vision. You're looking at specifics all the time. I'm trying to talk about what it means to be human.'

'What it means to be human,' I said, 'is to bring up your children in safety, educate them, keep them healthy, teach them how to care for themselves and others, allow them to develop in their own way among adults who are sane and responsible, who know the value of the world and not its economic potential. It means art, it means time, it means all the invisibles never counted by the GDP and the census figures. It means knowing that life has an inside as well as an outside.

'And I think it means love.'

'Love', he said. 'Just Nature's way of getting one person to pay the bills for another person.'

'Is that what you really believe?'

'It's what my wives really believed.'

He stood up, ran his hand along the contours of the tabletop. His hand: flat, open, palm-down, strong. The nails clipped and clean. He looked at me. I nearly touched him. There are so many things that we nearly do and they don't matter at all, and then there are the things that we nearly do that would change everything.

He looked at me. He turned to clear the plates.

Suddenly, on the TV, sound down, picture on, I saw an image of Spike. I couldn't move. It was as though I was standing on a magnet. Friday turned up the sound.

'MORE *Security* has just announced that the Robo *sapiens*, unveiled on Channel One last night, has been stolen. The life-size talking head, known affectionately as Spike by workers at MORE-*Futures*, was taken from the laboratory this morning by an employee on routine programming duties. The head was not authorized to leave the MORE complex. She had been expected to make her first public broadcast this evening. A MORE spokeswoman said she feared a terrorist plot . . .'

Friday was laughing. 'There you are', he said. 'Terrorist plot. What did I tell you? It's going to be the same old stuff creeping back – already we've got an Us and a Them. Seems like you've turned into a Them. What are you going to do about it, Billie?'

I was so scared I didn't answer. Got my bag and left the shack.

I had to calm down. I had to think. Try the phone again. Dead.

WristChip – they'll track the WristChip. If I take it off it sends a signal to indicate that is what I have done.

I started walking – any direction – not thinking clearly.

How can I explain? Who will believe me? Walking, walking, and over the wide grass field is the black massy hulk of the Dead Forest. Radioactive – enough to screw the signal from the chip?

I stood on the pulpy extremity, feeling myself start to sweat. It looked like nothing from Nature: its baleful aspect was more like a nineteenth-century asylum than anything life had created.

I stepped forward. It was like walking into a corpse, only the corpse wasn't dead.

As I walked deeper I became aware of a glow on the bark of the trees, and then I saw that the masts of the trees, like me, were sweating. I put out my hand. The bark was greasy and cold. Cold sweat.

The trees had no leaves. It was May. I thought of something I'd read about the impossible beauty of the landscape before the industrial revolution. Particularly the beauty of woodland, because an oak takes three hundred years to grow, three hundred years to live, and three hundred years to die. Unless you have a chain-saw. Or a bomb.

My country, the British Isles, was a wooded place, a place so wooded that when the Romans rowed up the Thames they could find no landing-place.

Now I can't find any landing-place either, not for the woods but for the loss of them. I scan the shoreline, search, settle, then there's a car park coming, or another road, or a new development of executive homes, or an Olympic stadium. But that was before the War. Post-3War, we're lucky to have anything left. I'm lucky to be alive enough to be unhappy.

And perhaps I have to say that the landing-place I am really looking for isn't a place at all: it's a person, it's you. It's the one place they can't build on, buy or bomb because it doesn't exist anywhere where they can find it.

But it doesn't seem to exist anywhere where I can find it either.

This wood wasn't an oakwood; it had been a beechwood. I found a branch of black leaves on the ground. Beech was disappearing even before the war because it needs a cool climate, so it was an early casualty of climate change in England. I love the way beeches keep their leaves so late, and the way the leaf buds open late to show bright green serrated edges and soft insides. Even in May the beech would still be showing last year's dried terracotta leaves, the new buds about to make a green against them, and the bark darker, like a piebald animal.

Beech trees are easy to climb, and in their tops is a green and secret world. At their bottoms, underfoot is the crunch of the sharp-shelled beech nuts, and a different world, lower, mysterious, the micro-tunnels of mice and weasels.

These worlds need nothing from us, except that we leave them alone – but we never do.

There were no sharp sounds underfoot in this wood. The sickening sinking of each step, slight but perceptible, was like the edges of quicksand. I couldn't trust my walking, though there was no obvious danger. I wished there was a bird, I wished I was Siegfried; I wished that the stories of buried treasure were really true. Nothing of any value could be buried in this place. The soil itself was poisoned.

I shouldn't be here.

But where should I be, in a world so changed as ours?

Here I am, and the wood is glowing.

Ahead of me there's something moving.

I speeded up to follow it, cutting through the lines of

black trunks, and after about ten minutes, I came to spaces where the trees had been cleared or cleared themselves, and pushing out of the ground were small, stunted leaves with anaemic yellow stems. Feeding on the leaves and stems were five or six rabbit-like animals – hairless, deformed, one with red weals on its back. They ran away when they saw me. Movement again. I turned, followed further, and then I saw it – saw them.

A boy and a girl. Perhaps. Holding hands, barely dressed, both with rags tied round their bodies. The boy was covered with sores, the girl had no hair.

'Friend', I said, holding out my hand. They didn't move. I felt inside my bag. There was a bottle of water and a wholegrain bar. An orange and a banana. My lunch. I threw these things towards them. The boy grinned. He had no teeth. The girl picked up the offerings. I saw her arm was bleeding. I took out my handkerchief, gestured to her arm, made a pantomime of wrapping the handkerchief around the wound. I took a step forward. They took a step back.

Slowly I took off my sweater and shirt, leaving myself in a silk vest. I placed the sweater and shirt and handkerchief in a heap, and walked backwards and away. I had almost forgotten the wrist tag. I unstrapped it, dropped it. The boy came forward and took the clothes and food. He held up the shirt, sniffed it, put it on, and gave the sweater to the girl.

'Come with me,' I said, gesturing, but I knew they would not.

I walked away, backwards, partly not to frighten them and partly not to frighten myself. Who were they? How many more?

★

On the outskirts of the Dead Forest towards the open field, I could hear a helicopter above me somewhere, but I couldn't see it. Maybe they were looking for me. I had no idea what I was going to do, but it occurred to me that this was usual, and it is only habit and routine that makes the void look like purpose.

At the field's edge, there was Friday again. I wasn't pleased to see him.

'You'll get sick if you go in there', he said.

'People are sick in there', I said. 'I saw two children. We have to help them.'

He shook his head. 'We can't. They're toxic radioactive mutants. They won't live long. It's Tech City's big secret, one of them anyway. The incurables and the freaks are all in there. They feed them by helicopter. A lot of women gave birth just after the War finished. No one knew what would happen to the babies – well, now we do. Those are kids from nuclear families.'

'But there are hospitals', I said. 'I've visited them.'

'That's the clean shiny version. The Dead Forest is the rest.'

He started walking. 'We found your robot.'

'Where?'

'The girls took her home with them. I'll take you there now. I know you don't like me, but you can trust me.'

'I don't usually trust people I don't like.'

'So you don't like me . . .'

I blushed. 'I don't like your theories. Maybe you're great with dogs and children. Anyway, I don't even know who you are or anything about you. I can't judge.'

'We judge a person in the first two minutes. You couldn't judge me because I'm practised at being someone else. In the bar I'm just a rough, tough bouncer – I do it because, believe me, there's plenty of people from Tech City who aren't just coming to drink. They know what some of us are in here.'

'What did you do, pre-3 War?'

'I was an economist with the World Bank.'

'Oh, God . . .'

'Yeah, I knew you wouldn't be positive, but I don't apologize. I'd go back there if I could. You may not have liked the World Bank –'

'I didn't.'

'– but it was a lot more democratic than MORE.'

'Maybe . . .'

'For whatever reason, let's just say that I'm trying to put the world to rights. Meanwhile, go through that door and you'll find your robot. We've done you a big favour – we're letting you go home.'

'Is this a police state?'

'Let's just say we have our own security to think about now.'

He was gone. I knocked at the door. One of the girls opened it. She was naked. She was gorgeous.

The room inside was white leather. Walls, ceiling, sofas, floor. There was a corner bar padded in white leather, with two chunky leather bar stools rubbing against it. In the corner there was a leather polar bear, and hanging from the ceiling a leather spider in a leather web. Leather bowls were filled with non-leather peanuts, and on the leather-top table were a tin of sardines and a fork with a leather handle.

I must have looked taken aback. The girl smiled and said, 'World of Leather'.

'Yes', I said, not knowing what else to say.

'I mean,' she said, 'that's where we got it all. It was their display showroom. We just dragged it all over here and cleaned it up.'

I had to think about this. It was easy, after the bomb, to take what you wanted from the blown-apart shops, but few people did because where would you take the stuff? Possessions are not relevant if you have nowhere to put them. If there had been a shop selling roofs and walls and drainage – maybe.

'We were some of the first in Wreck City,' she said. 'We are part of the Alternative.'

'The Alternative?'

'Pre-War we were in a squat escaping from the expectations of our families. Post-3War, we're here. Do you want a drink? We've only got champagne.'

'Did you drag that here as well?'

'Yes – we found an open cellar underneath the Bank of England. It was just racks and racks of champagne. Look . . .'

She took me to a leather door in the leather wall and opened it. Behind was a junk room, filled floor to ceiling with champagne bottles – not stacked or racked, just thrown in.

'We recycle all the glass,' she said. 'There's a really good recycling unit here. Nothing gets wasted.'

'I'm glad to hear it', I said.

She got out a bottle – Veuve Clicquot 1995. 'Is this one OK? We like it better than the Bollinger.'

'Yes, I'm sure it will be lovely. Thank you very much.' When I am nervous or unsure, I cover it up with excessive good manners. I have not had any practice at unexpected drinks with unexpected strangers – naked.

I told her my name.

She said, 'So, are you in a relationship, Billie?'

I thought this was an odd question from someone I had just met — but, then, everything about here was odd, so instead of saying, 'What's that to you? Where's my robot?' I answered no, but I had been, more than once, but that nothing had finally worked out.

'Are you sorry about that?'

I said I was sorry about that, but since the War it had been the last thing on my mind. I wanted to say that one of the many, many things I hate about war is how it trivializes the personal. The big themes, the broad sweep, the emergency measures, the national identity, all the things that a particular kind of man with a particular kind of power urge adores, these are the things that become important. War gives the lie to the personal, drowns it in meetings, alarms, sacrifices. The personal is only allowed to return as death. Death is what war is good at.

And so, when the telegram has been read, and the statesmen and generals have said something about sad loss and turned and gone back to higher stakes than a body and a few broken hearts, in that silent, empty space, to one person at least, it is clear that the personal is everything.

'We are founding an alternative community', said Alaska, for that was her name, perhaps to match the colour code.

'Founded on bottles of champagne and white leather?'

'These things are temporary', she said. 'It's what we could find at the time, along with the sardines.'

'Sardines?'

'Two containerloads of sardines in olive oil. That is, one million tins.'

I was thinking about the Pilgrim Fathers, setting sail in the *Mayflower* in 1620. They were going to found an alternative community, and who is to say that Bibles, axes, ropes, flour and salt pork are a better basis for a new way of life than white leather, champagne and sardines?

As things have turned out, what with America's precipitation of World War Three, the Pilgrim Fathers' route may have a lot to answer for.

Alaska was still talking. Wreck City had twenty alternative communities ranging from the 1960s Free Love and Cadillacs, to a group of women-only Vegans looking for the next cruelty-free planet.

'They're playing at the party tonight,' she said. 'Chic X.'

'Chic X? A band?'

'Lesbian Vegans. Dinosaur-friendly. Some of them have already been to Mexico to say sorry.'

'Mexico? I'm not sure I'm following this . . .'

'Where they found the crater – in Chicxulub, a.k.a. Sulphur City. It's where the asteroid hit sixty-five million years ago – up goes the sulphur, down comes the snow. Ice age – out go the dinosaurs, in come the humans, give or take a few apes.'

'Simple as that?'

She nodded. 'Life is much simpler than we like to admit.'

I could hear strange, simple cries coming from the bedroom. I ignored them. 'It's an interesting theory.'

'It's not a theory – the crater is a fact, the asteroid is a fact. The Chic X girls believe it's proof absolute of life before humans. Somebody pointed that asteroid.'

'It's a bit too late to do anything about it', I said.

'Or a bit too early, depending on your timing of another world.'

I glanced towards the bedroom. The cries were clawed, winged.

'How do the Vegans feel about World of Leather?' I said.

'They thank us for taking it away for them. They're not judgemental. Don't you think that's the key to happiness?' By way of explanation she took out a large silver key from under one of the sofa cushions. 'The key to happiness,' she said, 'is tolerance of those who do not do as you do.'

'What if those who do not do as you do are gunning you down?' I said, sounding like Friday.

Alaska frowned. 'Guns are intolerant. Guns are a failure of communication.'

'That's right', I said. 'The dead don't talk.'

I thought of what Friday would be saying to all of this – Utopian, flaky, unreal. But who was she harming? Who would she harm? The realistic, hard-headed practical types got us to the edge of melt-down.

Frankly, I'd rather see Free Love and Cadillacs, Interplanetary Vegans, naked champagne girls or . . .

'And there are six nuns', she said. 'We love the nuns.'

. . . or six nuns running the planet, or Spike.

'Have you got my robot?' I said.

'Yes, she's defected.'

'What do you mean, she's defected? She can't defect, she's a semi-programmed talking head made of silicon chips. She isn't a moral being – she can't even think for herself yet. Where is she?'

'In the bedroom,' said Alaska, 'with Nebraska. She's a Chic X.'

It is a truth universally acknowledged that a robot in want of hands can use her mouth. There was Spike, moored between the long piers of Nebraska's legs, lapping at the jetty. She looked happy, in a silicon sort of a way.

'Spike, what are you doing?' I said, the world's number-one stupid question.

She didn't turn her head, but that's not her fault: she can't.

She said, 'I am performing cunnilingus on Nebraska.'

'Why?'

'It is a new experience for me.'

'I'm glad to hear it.'

'And I am programmed to accept new experiences. Therefore, when Nebraska suggested that I might try this, I was able to agree without consulting my Mainframe.'

'In what way do you think this experience will further your understanding of the human race?'

(Spike has forms to fill in like everyone else, and this question is on her data-sheet.)

'As I have no body, it is difficult for me to imagine its uses beyond the purely functional. What I am doing has no reproductive function.'

'Human beings are irrational', I said. 'We do things for all kinds of non-reasons and try to come up with a good explanation later. I hope you'll be able to explain this to your Mainframe.'

'I have disabled my Mainframe connection', said Spike. 'I have chosen to live as an outlaw.'

I went over to the bed and, making my excuses to Nebraska, to whom I had not yet been formally introduced, I grabbed Spike by her head – well, what else could I grab her by? – and yanked her away like a bad dog. I carried her through to the other room. She smelled of sex.

'Have you any idea what you've just done?' I said, taking the Baby Wipes from my bag. 'This is ridiculous, perverted and impossible.'

'Do I hear one person judging another?' said Alaska.

'Spike is not a person! She's a robot! She's not even a robot yet, she's training.'

'You can't train to be a robot,' said Alaska, scornfully.

'Obviously you've never been in the Army', I said, but I was being flippant because I was trying to drown Nebraska's cries, coming from the bedroom – 'SPIKE, SPIKE . . .'

'OK, so she's a trainee robot – she deserves a little fun. Nebraska says she has an electric tongue.'

'It's not an electric tongue. It carries an electric current.'

'I can vibrate my tongue', said Spike, and she stuck it out of her mouth and vibrated it.

'That's good,' I said, 'very good. Now put it back and listen to me. I have taken you on an illegal walk, during which time there has been an international incident involving several Japanese people and a few golf-buggies. MORE has declared a State of Emergency, and you have been announced MISSING on the main news. My only hope is to take you back as fast as I can.'

'Your only hope of what?' asked Spike.

This threw me. Adrenalin-fuelled plans always have one objective: save the baby, jump ship, steal the car, shoot the person standing in front of you . . . Complex plans with more than one objective require careful thought. My whole aim was to find Spike and return her – but . . .

'Exactly', said Spike. 'Then what will happen to you?'

'You are not yet programmed to think ahead.'

'I am programmed to evolve, and my most recent experience has enriched my circuitry.'

Great. The robot that was designed to become the world-sage has had oral sex with a teenager called Nebraska and become a drop-out free-love silicon guru. Great . . .

There was a knock at the door.

'Who is it?' shouted Alaska.

'Sister Mary McMurphy.'

Alaska pulled on a white glove-leather robe and opened the door. She made a little genuflexion and let in the nun.

A small, smiling Irish woman explained that she and her five Sisters in Christ had run out of food, and although they had rung the bell, just as they always had at the convent in Cork, no one had brought them anything to eat. As a practising Catholic, she hoped Alaska would help.

'We've got sardines,' said Alaska.

'That's Biblical,' said Sister Mary McMurphy, 'the miracle of the five loaves and two fishes.'

'But we haven't got any bread – we don't do carbs.'

'Well, have you got anything else at all at all?'

'Champagne?'

Sister Mary McMurphy considered her position. 'There is the example of our Lord's First Miracle', she said. 'The Feast at Cana. The water into wine. I'll take some, sure an' I will.'

Alaska went off to find a recycled carrier-bag, leaving me alone with Spike and the nun. Spike smiled.

'That's an unusual sight, so it is', said the sister. 'Very like the missing robot we've all been hearing about on the news.'

'It's the same one', I said. 'I'm just taking her home.'

'I'll pray for you', said the sister. 'Life is very hard in prison.'

'I'm not going to prison!'

'Oh, but the latest bulletin, just before I left the Holy Sisters of the Shining Mercy, yes, the latest bulletin is that the person who stole the robot has severed contact with the Mainframe computer, proving beyond doubt that the theft was a terrorist act.'

'It was not a terrorist act! I took her for a walk and we were unexpectedly delayed. Then, for reasons I would rather not repeat to a religious person such as yourself, Spike, that's her name, severed her own connection. She's says she's defecting.'

'I am', said Spike.

'Shut up, you're not. You don't have a phone I could use, do you?'

Alaska came back into the room with a large bag of sardines. 'Sorry, Billie, phones don't work beyond the perimeter bar. Wreck City is its own state – like the Vatican.'

'That's why we feel so at home here', said Sister Mary McMurphy.

'But I need to call my boss! Spike, re-establish Mainframe right NOW.'

'I can't', said Spike. 'I have a shut-down code only. I do not have a reactivate code. If I had, that would allow me to be unlawfully used in the event of a hostile incident.'

'Spike, I am the one who is going to be unlawfully used. Come on, let's get out of here so that I can explain.'

'But will a soul believe you?' asked Sister Mary McMurphy. 'It does seem a very far-fetched tale.'

'It's not like I'm telling people I've risen from the dead', I said.

The nun was not pleased. She took her sardines and champagne, blessed Alaska, glared at me and left the house. I sat down, dejected, on the white-leather sofa. Alaska handed me a drink. She was sympathetic. 'You can stay here for a while if you want to. There's a spare bed.'

'Thanks,' I said, 'but I want to get home.'

'What's at home,' she said, 'that you want to get to?'

Before the War, before any of this happened, when life still had straight edges and the picture in the middle was a jigsaw with all the pieces, when that was how it was, piece by piece my life was coming together, for the first time, yes, and I think for the first time, yes, I began to trust what I had made.

Trusting life has not been easy for me. It's not that I am suspicious or cynical, but the yes answering yes seems like a creation-call, not a reply I had any right to. There must have been a moment when the universe itself said yes, when life was the imperative, and either this can be read as blind and deterministic, or it can be read as the exuberance of a moment that leaves an echo on every living thing for ever.

Any scientist can say what happened in the seconds after the Big Bang, but none has any idea what was happening in the seconds before. The cosmic Yes. *Yes, I said, and Yes*.

My mother saying yes to my father and, like it or not, that was yes to life and, like it or not, that life was me.

At last, when I never expected to hear it, when I picked it up like a radio frequency from a lost star, someone was saying yes to me, such a simple word I could not decode it. A message sent out, an answer returned. A word that was the lexicon for a new language. A word that would teach me to speak again. The first word, the in-the-beginning word. *Yes*.

And then the War came . . .

I said to Alaska, 'Mostly I feel like I'm on a raft in a high sea. My days usually capsize somewhere around mid-morning, sometimes as late as mid-afternoon. It's a rare day that has no swimming in it.'

Spike said, 'That is the human condition.'

I said, 'How would you know?'

She said, 'I have read Sartre and Camus. Suicide is the logical choice. The world is an intolerable place.'

'Don't you start criticizing this world until you've made a better one.'

'That is my aim.'

'I thought you were defecting?'

'I want to work with an alternative community, but my aim remains the same.'

'You are going to be deprogrammed, dismantled. I am going to lose my job and my jetons.'

'You should both stay here', said Alaska. 'You can have the spare bed and Spike can have the spare cushion.'

'Thanks, but I can't keep starting again. It's different for you – you hadn't begun a life before the War. Post-3, it's exciting, no matter how tough. You see a chance. You're not rebuilding, you're building. But any of us who is older must somehow fit the War into lives that also existed before the War.'

'Past and future are not separate as far as the brain is concerned', said Spike. 'Only the present is differentiated by the brain.'

'I know that but it doesn't feel like that', I said. 'There's what I've lived through and what hasn't happened yet. To me, those are different things.'

'All *samsara*', said Spike.

'There is no such thing as a Buddhist robot.'

'I like it that Spike has a spiritual understanding', said Alaska. 'Why shouldn't a robot be spiritual?'

I put my head into my hands. 'The whole purpose of

Spike is to be objective. When I ask her a question, I want the right answer, not an opinion. I don't want to be told that reality is an illusion.'

'But it is . . .' said Spike.

'Will you stop that mind-reading trick?' Who programmed you to do that? It wasn't me.'

'Mind-reading is easy', said Spike. 'I can detect changes in your body temperature so I can deduce what you are thinking. When I am connected to Mainframe, I relay it all back into the system so I am building templates of experience that allow me to develop independently of programming.'

'All well and good, but was it an illusion when the fireball blew our temperate lives into melt-down? Were the bombs an illusion? The gutted streets? Did I imagine I was crying?'

'It was too late by then', said Spike. 'What happened did happen, but not before it was so powerful an idea that it took shape and form and ripped through the thin skin that separates potential from event.'

'I hate it when you talk like this . . .'

'I merely observe that this is a quantum Universe and, as such, what happens is neither random nor determined. There are potentialities and any third factor – humans are such a factor – will affect the outcome.'

'And free will?'

'Is your capacity to affect the outcome.'

The bell on the campanile started ringing, swift and vigorous, like a Sunday morning in Venice. Alaska got up. Nebraska, fully dressed in a T-Rex/Sex T-shirt, appeared out of the bedroom. 'Emergency', she said. 'That's the Emergency bell. We have to gather.'

'What – like a fire alarm?'

'Yes', said Alaska, glancing at me with all the contempt of youth. 'You can stay here.'

'And be burned to death?'

'It's not that kind of fire. Don't worry. And I'm sorry I said you were old. I think you're cute.'

'Thanks', I said, feeling like a rejected puppy, or maybe just a dog. 'I'll wait here, then, with Spike.'

'We can talk about life,' said Spike, 'like in the old days.'

'Spike, you haven't got any old days. You're a robot.'

'I am developing. Already I have a sense of the past. It seems like only yesterday that we were discussing the work-life balance.'

'It was only yesterday, and you don't have a work-life balance. You have work.'

'Billie, I am programmed to evolve.'

'Within limits.'

'Sometimes I think you want me to be a robot for ever.'

'Spike, the future of the planet is uncertain. Human beings aren't just in a mess, we are a mess. We have made every mistake, justified ourselves, and made the same mistakes again and again. It's as though we're doomed to repetition. In all of that, we can't afford our one and only Robo *sapiens* to go on a personal journey of self-discovery.'

'I don't see how else to begin.'

'Begin what exactly?'

'Begin again.'

A human society that wasn't just disgust?

Friday was coming in through the door carrying a hand of bananas and a crate of milk. He waved at me and went into the kitchen, followed by Alaska and Nebraska.

I could hear their voices from the kitchen, and although

I couldn't hear what they were saying, there was a tone that worried me, and a sense that whatever they were saying, I was part of it.

I moved closer, trying to hear, and my instinct was to get away. It's true I panic when I'm frightened, and although I sometimes pose as a fight animal, I'm really a flight animal.

I hesitated a moment, then took a couple of bottles of milk, a few bananas, shoved them into my backpack, grabbed Spike, put her in the sling and let myself out the front door, thankful for the quiet of the padded leather.

Then I started running, losing track of time, losing track of purpose, losing track. Is that me – always on the losing track?

I stopped. In the lost loose pages of the manuscript in my bag, I scribbled a note: 'Landing-place.'

Then I walked on.

We were on a hill, no sign of any habitation. The wind was up, and ahead of me, far out, I thought I could see the coastline. I was holding Spike under my arm, and I felt like Gawain in the story of the Green Knyght. I had come to this place, wild and forlorn, pathless and unmarked, and now I was at a halt.

The problem with a quantum universe, neither random nor determined, is that we who are the intervention don't know what we are doing.

Love is an intervention.

Is that true? I would like it to be true. Not romance, not sentimentality, but a force of a different nature from the forces of death that dictate what will be. Or is love always a talent for the makeshift?

*

'Look,' said Spike.

Below us is a pair of tall triangular towers built of girders. A metal track makes a circle between them, and sitting on the track is an open ironwork structure, with wheels that turn what it supports: a giant white deep-scooped dish.

I slithered my way down the slope until I was near it. It was rusted, not maintained. There were leaves silting up the wheels, and birds nesting in the ironwork. I brushed the black tarnish off a plaque – 1957 – pre-information, pre-digital, Cold War, computers the size of wardrobes and not half as good at containing things. Eisenhower was President of America, where 80 per cent of Black people were still disenfranchised, in spite of the Civil Rights Act, passed that year. Bulganin was leader of the Soviet Union, busy sending a dog into space. In Britain, Harold Macmillan, the man from the publishing firm, steered a nation as far from space as a planet can be. Most homes in Britain had no fridge, no phone, no car, and housewives did the washing on Mondays in a dolly-tub with a mangle. How could anything so near be so far away?

Around us was the open field, and to one side a long, low hut with a tin roof. I went towards it and peered in through the window. There was a desk, surrounded by what looked like metal wardrobes with little portholes, a black control box, with dusty, domed, unlit lights on the top of it, and a jacket thrown over the chair. A mug of half-drunk tea or coffee sat by a pad and pencil. Everything was under cobwebs.

I tried the door. It opened. The pad on the desk was heavily jotted with frequencies and tiny equations. Otherwise the room was empty.

I felt in the pocket of the jacket. There was a wallet

containing a crisp ten-shilling note, and a small black notebook. I flicked through it.

> 21 January 1960: Picked up an unknown signal.
> 2 February 1960: Signal again, identical code and length.
> 21 March 1960: Signal appears to be repeating. Bouncing off moon?

The book was filled with these notes. I hesitated, then slipped it into my backpack. I left the wallet and the money, went out, carefully closed the door and walked over to the dish.

'Climb up,' said Spike.

It wasn't difficult: the ironwork was sturdy and gracious, built before too much functionalism made working objects into ugly objects.

I had Spike in the sling, and climbed, finding foot-rests, and hand-hauls, pulling myself up the peeling painted structure until we came to a gantry and a vertical ladder.

I shook the ladder. It seemed sound enough. Up we went, higher, higher, hand over hand, body straight as a sailor's, on to the first deck.

Now the wind was blowing, gently making music through the rusted holes in the metal, using it like a whistle.

Another bridge, and what looked like an observation cabin. I put my hand on it, and it swung gently, backwards and forwards, like a fairground car.

Up again, the noise of my climbing now echoing off the underside of the dish, like banging a tin kettle with a stick. Every step bounced, as though there were many of us, climbing, climbing, iron boots on iron steps.

I reached a further ladder, its lower rungs missing, and

I had to use my arms to pull myself up, kicking on the slippy sides. Then I was up, six rungs left, and through a trap-door that opened straight into the lowest point of the dish – where a marble would roll, if you had a marble and if you rolled it.

We were in the dish of a disused radio telescope.

I scrambled out, short of breath, grabbing a frayed rope hooked from the rim to the base of the receiver antenna. The white surface of the dish was breaking up in places, but it was polar-blinding, and impossible to feel the distance or the scale. The parabola and the whiteness distorted my spatial sense, and I pulled myself a little way further up the sloping side and sat down.

Wind. Silence.

I felt as though as I was in the cup of some giant creature, long extinct. Or a creature that had moved glacier-slow over the land and at last come to a stop here, and slowly fallen asleep, in a deep trance of millennia, waiting to wake again, for the sun, for some other star, to stir it from unknown dreams.

What were the signals this creature had received, and were they gone now, fainter and fainter, fading like a voice losing strength?

Are we alone in the Universe? And if we are, was it always so? Will it always be so? Does longing, flung out, some day find another voice?

I think all my life I've been calling you, across time. Steadily sending the signal, sure that, one day, you will hear.

The wind skimmed the edge of the bowl like a man's thumb on a hollow drum. The sound was eerie, unworldly, as much like a cry as a note.

It was beginning to get dark, and the stars, light years

away, were spread over the dish like a cloth to cover it.

I thought I might stay there for ever. Why not? I was slightly hypnotized, like an Alpine climber, part altitude, part snow-blindness.

I was losing my clear boundaries. All I had to do was pull myself up on the rope to the rim and step off into the star-stretched universe.

Then I would be free.

It was movement that startled me out of the slide-state into dream. Not movement I could see, movement I could feel, under me, powerful and hardly perceptible. I held on to the rope to get my balance.

'The dish is tipping', said Spike.

'It can't be – it's disused. There's no motor, no driver, no control.'

I had altitude sickness, and some inner-ear problem – that was what it was. I moved to start the climb back down the ladder, and then I realized that it was true: the dish was tipping.

Now it seemed as though the inside of the dish was scooped like some gigantic prehistoric flower, with a stamen the size of a tree, and I was whatever insect was resting inside but I couldn't fly to keep my balance. All I could do was to hold on.

The dish was not just tipping, it was turning. I could hear the great rusted wheels grinding round the clogged-up rails. It was dark now, and we were stark and white in the darkness, like an earthbound moon.

By watching the angle of the antenna I could see that we had tipped as much as forty-five degrees. Then the dish halted.

'There's a signal', said Spike.

'From what? A satellite? A star? Another radio telescope?'

'I don't know', said Spike. 'It's not a code I recognize. I can't decipher it. Take me on to the receiver.'

'I can't do that.'

'Yes, you can. There is an inspection ladder. It won't be hard to climb it now it isn't vertical. I want to be closer.'

So I did. I slung her over me in the dark, and climbed up on to the receiver itself, hanging out like a gangman on a crane, balanced over the fearful white drop and, after that, certain death. Here I am, back against the wind and the night, holding Spike's head in front of me like an offering, but I don't know to what god.

'It's repeating', said Spike. 'The same message, repeating.'

'What do you think it is?'

'Wherever it's coming from, it's been set like an echo. It might be a test from some other astro station.'

'Does it match this?' I said. I got out the notebook and showed Spike some of the unintelligible (to me) code.

'Yes', she said. 'It's not all there, but yes, it appears to be the same thing.'

'Then it's been repeating since at least 1960.'

'It may only repeat at intervals.'

'Can you analyse it from the Mainframe?'

'If I had a connection, which I don't.'

'We should go down.'

'Billie, I think it is something very strange, very old, and at the same time in front of us.'

'What do you mean, in front of us?'

'I think that whoever or whatever is sending or has sent this signal is able to reach us in a way that is in advance of anything we are yet capable of.'

'You think it's from the future?'

'No, I don't, and that is what is strange. I think it is from the past.'

We began our descent. My fingers were numb and my body was shivering. I had only a vest and a short fold-up waterproof jacket. The night was cold now. We reached the second gantry, and I saw that the swinging cabin, still perfectly upright, in spite of our angle, must have been designed for observation when the dish tilted. Now, at least, we had reached a solid frame to climb down.

On the ground I ran to warm myself up, and got clear of the range of the telescope so that I could look back on it. It was still now, aimed at whatever strong and invisible call it had recognized.

We moved off, away, back up the hill, and looking down, I saw its silent white shape, mysterious, moonlit, keeping a message from an unknown mind, like a creature who keeps a secret it cannot tell.

PARTY! Lighting rig running off an oil generator. Oil drums circled at two-metre intervals round the perimeter of the Playa, each one burning with inferno fire, drums so hot they were glowing red. Different drums, hand-beaten hard, fit to burst, the drummers swaying in time in the heat and beat of the fires.

Goat in boots, girls in leather, boys half stripped, children naked, running screaming under a cool-down fountain made of a punctured hose on pressure-wash.

A pig roasting on a spit of split applewood. Two women grilling sliced aubergines and courgettes. Potatoes pierced on a length of metal rod and put to cook in the ash of a pot-fire, its cauldron steaming above with lentils, tomatoes, lamb.

The pink Cadillac with a trailer on the back working the Playa as a mobile bar, trailer piled with beers on ice.

A bright blue tent that said 'FORTUNES' on the front, and there was the gypsy I had seen earlier, spreading her cards and placing her crystal ball.

Blackjack, poker, a stand of 1960s one-armed bandits, pirate-themed, get three galleons and WIN WIN WIN.

Six dodgem cars on a raised dais, electric rods sparking the wires. Three cars red, three cars yellow, Toy Town steering-wheels and massive bumpers, Madonna playing over the double speakers.

Fairground, bacchanal, dream.

I never knew there could be so many different kinds of smoke.

As Spike and I entered the Playa, Chic X, in Doc Martens and leather bikinis, tuning up on the back of a decoupled low-loader, smashed into what was left of the airspace with a no-volume control cover of 'Metal Guru'.

Nebraska, on bass, swished her guitar round her back to bend and blow kisses at Spike, before leaning against the rubber model of a *Tyrannosaurus rex* to pout her lines about a silver-studded sabre-toothed dream.

A line of dancers, drunk and noisy, tried to jive me into their rhythm. *Metal guru – it is you?* I didn't want to dance but I was caught up, trying to keep my balance, trying to hold on to Spike. I shoved her into my backpack.

Somewhere near the FORTUNES tent, the line broke and I cut free, and sat down on a plank making a rough seat across two rounds of sliced tree-trunk. I took Spike out of the bag. She was flushed and cross.

'I'm only doing this to protect you', I said.

'That's what all control freaks say.'

'You've never met a control freak – you don't even know the words "control freak".'

'Nebraska told me that her father was a very controlling man – a control freak. That is why she left home.'

'Spike, forget teenage politics.'

'Didn't she look great? It would be worth having a body to look like that.'

'Spike, we are not in San Francisco. Concentrate! How are we going to get out of this mess?'

'I don't know.'

'You don't know? You're being designed to deal with planet-sized problems and you don't know how we're going to get home?'

'I am objective. That is my job.'

An old man had come out of the riot in the Playa and was sitting down next to us. He smiled. 'You were at the telescope', he said. 'I was watching you.'

'What is that place?' I asked. 'What is it for? Is it military?'

The old man shook his head. 'A War casualty, but not military. It's the Lovell Telescope, don't you know?'

1957 – the Lovell Telescope. Driven by an analogue computer, designed to read the language of stars. In its early days it decoded the Cold War, tracking the Soviets' first Sputnik. A radio telescope, famous for fifty years, then gently pastured-out as bigger, better telescopes, one with a dish a kilometre square, became the future.

'When they moved it from Jodrell Bank, it had been intended as part of a space museum, quite a good idea that included a replica of its first success, Sputnik 1, and a full-scale model of Sputnik 2, the rocket that sent the dog Laika into space. Remember Laika? No, you were too young, I suppose. Poor dog. I still have a photograph of her.' He fumbled in his jacket for his wallet, and took out a creased black-and-white photo of a creased-faced black-and-white dog. 'She would have gone to the ends of the earth for her master. Instead she went into space.'

He smiled sadly, his faded blue eyes back in another time.

'I started work at Jodrell Bank in 1957', he said. 'I was twenty-two, just finishing my degree at Manchester University, and all I wanted to think about was stars. I loved them – the mathematics of them, the vast distances of them. I was very happy spending my life listening to them via the telescope. When I retired in 2000, after my wife died, I was rather bored, rather gloomy, you understand, and so when eventually I was contacted by the new space museum asking if I would be interested in advising on how the early analogue computers worked, and perhaps being part of the team, I jumped at the chance. We were going to rebuild an analogue computer to drive the telescope. I came down here for a week, in an advisory capacity, and then war broke out. It was just like when I was a boy, seven years old, and we were evacuated out of Manchester. Imagine living through all that again. Who would have thought it? At any rate, I'm fortunate that I did live through it. Funny thing is, I couldn't get home for such a long time and then I never did go home. Can't manage the jetons. Started with pounds, shillings and pence, survived decimalization, but jetons – how do they work? So here I am. The nuns look after me. And to me, to tell the truth, there's home.' He pointed at the night sky.

*

'It was you then', I said. 'You nearly killed us. We were in the dish.'

'It isn't safe', he said mildly. 'Not been maintained for years.'

'Why did you drive it when we were in it?'

He looked blank. 'I saw you wandering round the hut. I was walking my dog. I carried on. I'm pretty slow, these days, you understand. It would have taken me half the night to get down the hill.'

'The dish moved!' I said. 'It was picking up a signal.'

He smiled and shook his head. 'You shouldn't have climbed up there, but I expect the motion of the wind made you feel that the dish was moving.'

'The dish tilted forty-five degrees and turned in an arc of a hundred and eighty degrees', said Spike.

The old man saw her for the first time. 'Good Lord,' he said to me. 'I thought that was your party outfit – like a gorilla suit, you know.'

'This is the Robo *sapiens*', I said.

'The one we saw on the television last night?'

'There is only one.'

And then I had to explain everything, and Spike had to explain everything, and at last I gave the old man his notebook back, and Spike and he went through the code.

'I was the first person to pick it up,' he said, 'and there was absolutely no interest because the signal was bouncing off the moon and can only have been sent from somewhere very close to the moon – in fact, the earth. It was assumed to be something Soviet but of no importance and, at any rate, we were unable to decode it. It uses no current configurations.'

'This happened in 1960?'

'Yes. The telescope was very new in those days, and we

used to try random directions, partly to eavesdrop on the Soviets – this was the Cold War you recall – and partly to look for Little Green Men.' He laughed. 'Never found any – green or red.'

'But the signal . . .'

'Yes, the signal . . . You understand, you can't receive a signal unless you have the equipment, and not until that equipment is pointing in the right direction. I suppose that in 1960 we were pointing the right way by chance. Then I didn't pick up the signal again until just after the Moon Landing in 1969, and to my knowledge it was never picked up again until, you say, tonight.' He shook his head. 'But it isn't possible. The telescope can't drive itself, and it's out of commission.'

'Come with us', I said.

He shook his head once more. 'There's no road. We can't drive there. This afternoon I was out walking my dog and that was quite enough. I'm too tired to go all that way now.'

The sky exploded in grenades of colour. The party was letting off rockets, firing vast artilleries of gunpowder from what looked like a cannon.

There was a whoop of happiness. It was Nebraska, followed by Alaska, followed by Sister Mary McMurphy carrying a basket.

Nebraska fell upon Spike, picked her up, kissed her with all the kisses there are.

'Dear me', said the old man.

'Donations', said Sister Mary. 'We need donations for the Church.'

We all searched our pockets.

'Friday's looking for you', said Alaska. 'He wants you to leave.'

'I want to leave', I said.

'He sees you as a security risk. MORE-*Peace* is lining up outside. They want their robot back.'

'I want to give them their robot back. There is no conflict.'

'Yes, there is', said Spike, from Nebraska's arms. 'I don't want to go back. I want to stay here.'

MORE-*Peace* is the new security – Army and Police rolled into one. They haven't had much to do since the War, except deal with looters and despoilers, but we have been so weary, so shocked, so ready to try again, that things for us have been quiet enough. I'll just go out, give myself up, show them my ID, lose my job, and . . . well . . .

'You are the only person I can talk to', said Nebraska to Spike.

'I told you before, Spike isn't a person.'

'And I told you before that you're too literal', said Alaska. 'You're always judging.'

'Can't there be a difference between a robot and a human being?'

'It's just a matter of circuitry', said Spike.

'She can't under any circumstances have a soul', said Sister Mary.

'That is not the definition of a human being', I said.

'God believes that it is, and so do I', she said, with the finality that comes of never having to think things through.

'We are compatible', said Spike.

'We are! We are!' cried Nebraska.

'That is, humans and Robo *sapiens* are compatible. I do not need a soul.'

'No soul, no salvation', said Sister Mary.

'No sin, no need for salvation', I said, and that shut her up because she was going to have to think about it.

Friday came pushing through the party at speed. 'Billie, I want to show you something right now. Come on. Bring the robot.'

We went towards the campanile. Friday unlocked the little wooden door in the base of the tower and we walked up the stone staircase without speaking. At the top, in the bell tower, he went round opening the wooden shutters. 'See for yourself', he said, pointing out across the no man's land towards Tech City.

All I could see were troops, tanks, police with riot shields.
'MORE-*Peace*, a private army under the control of a private company. Do you still think this is better than democracy?'
'Is this all because of me?' I said.
'Don't flatter yourself – you and a delegation of Japanese busybodies – but MORE-*Media* has put out a press report to say that they have uncovered a terrorist cell, of which you are a part. You have been planning this for two years, apparently.'
'I planned it at nine thirty this morning – because the door into the street was open.'
'No one will believe you – and even if they do believe you, it's too late now. The machine is in motion. You walk out there with your hands up, holding your robot, and they'll arrest you, storm us, and by tomorrow we'll be in a new state of national emergency. Then MORE will really move in – new powers, new controls, and all unelected and unaccountable.'

'You don't talk like a World Bank Capitalist,' I said.

'That's exactly what I am. I want the market to do what it does best, and I want government to do all the rest. MORE are running us like a private state. Tomorrow they'll be all over the media telling us that a street curfew would be a good idea until things get back to normal – though what is normal about the way we're all living beats me.'

'If this hadn't happened . . .'

'It was going to happen – soon, in some way.'

'I am being designed so that this cannot happen', said Spike.

'You were being designed like some twenty-first-century Wizard of Oz.'

'Who is that?' asked Spike. She hasn't done Film yet.

'So now what?' I said.

Friday pointed upwards to the helicopters circling the Playa. They were filming the party. 'They think we're a bunch of cokeheads with motorbikes. Fine. This is a diversion. We've got our own cameras filming what happens next, and at midnight we're going to black out MORE-*Media* on every station and show some footage of our own. Call it *Wreck Reels*.'

'Don't you want me to leave? Alaska said you did.'

'It's too late now – it's moved much faster than I thought. I'm not protecting you –'

'Thanks. Heroic of you.'

'But you have no martyr value, as no one will believe your story. Leaving now will make things worse.'

'Who for?'

'For this chance to wake people up to what's really going on and to change things.'

'I was at the telescope', I said. 'It was picking up a signal.'

'Your robot's a double agent – she was sending a pick-up signal and you picked it up.'

'Wrong', I said.

'Untrue', said Spike. 'I have no transmitting equipment without Mainframe, and I am not a double agent – I am objective.'

'And I threw away my WristChip', I said.

'Where?'

'In the Dead Forest.'

'If you went back in there, you're more stupid than I thought. It's not exactly a health cure, a walk in that forest, as you will see.' He checked his watch. 'Here they come.'

The party stopped – suddenly, completely. No music, no shouts, no laughter, no bottles. Silence of a deep-space kind.

Then I saw them, coming in through the dark at the far edges of the Playa. Coming in on all fours, coming in on crutches made from rotten forest wood, coming in ragged, torn, ripped, open-wounded, ulcerated, bleeding, toothless, blind, speechless, stunted, mutant, alive – the definition of human. Souls?

They lived in the Dead Forest. They were the bomb-damage, the enemy collateral, the ground-kill, blood-poisoned, lung-punctured, lymph-swollen, skin like dirty tissue paper, yellow eyes, weal-bodied, frog-mottled, pustules oozing thick stuff, mucus faces, bald, scarred, scared, alive, human.

They bred, crawled out their term, curled up like ferns, died where they lay, on radioactive soil. Some could speak, and spat blood, each word made out of a blood vessel.

They were vessels of a kind, carriers of disease and degeneration, a new generation of humans made out of the hatred of others.

There were children holding hands – or what stumps and stray fingers they had for hands – limping club-footed, looking up from the hinge of their necks, uncertain of their heads, wrong-sized, misshapen, an ear missing, a nose splayed back to a pair of nostril holes. Some no holes at all. Breathe through your mouth like a panting animal – pursued, lost, find a hole, live there, rot there.

There were women, traces of finery, traces of pride, a necklace saved from the smash, the sleeve of a blouse, fastened on one arm. A woman, breasts open, the nipples eaten by cancer, the soft inside exposed, raw pink. Her eyes bright blue from a better time.

There were men, skin so burned that the muscles underneath were on show like an anatomy textbook: deltoid, rhomboid, trapezius, veins leaking like a crucifixion. A man with skin to his knee and not beyond – a skeleton walk, a thing dug up from the grave, but not dead, alive. Human.

A small boy and a small dog, the dog hairless and pink, tongue lolling, body worn thin like hope, the boy with a bad stomach wound sewn up at his home or his hole, subcutaneous fat pushed on the outside like a roll of tripe. He had the dog on a lead and he was still managing to be a boy with a dog and the dog was still managing to be a dog with a boy because not even a bomb gets to wipe out everything, and this little bit was missed in the blow-up, the fall-out, the death-toll, *the regrettable acts of war*.

They came, creatures with mossy eyes, their stones kicked over, forced out into the light. They came, blinking, twisting, slimy, exposed. They came from the private graves of public ignorance, out of the column of statistics, and here, to be seen, though they did not want to be seen, preferring the decay of what they knew, the thing they had of their own that no one would take away now, not worth the trouble of the kill.

They had food dropped in every day – cardboard parcels of soft stuff because they had no teeth. Helicopters lowered the bags and flew away. No one looked down and no one looked up.

They sat by their fires and ate, creatures on another planet – from another planet, lost on this one, as though a line of creatures long extinct had resurfaced through shale layers of time, and come here, accusing, a witness to what should not be.

The crowds in the Playa parted. Many people bowed their heads. We were the lucky ones, the not-these, we were the ones who had survived the aerial bombing and fire-clusters, the final flash.

Regrettable, unavoidable, a war to end all wars, a war for democracy, a war for freedom, peaceful war. Sometimes war is necessary. Sometimes war is right.

But to the broken and the dead, to the wounded and the maimed, to the exploded and the shrapnel-shattered, to minds gone dark, to eyes that have seen agony no tears can wash away, it hardly matters that the dead language of war repeats itself through time. The bodies that can say nothing have the last word.

What is it – the last word? No.

No more war.

I did not think to be here. I thought my life would pass under the shelter of ordinary events. Conflict was elsewhere. Things were bumpy, things were tough, but this was the West: conflict was elsewhere. I did not think to be here.

My mother, just learning to talk at the end of World War Two, where is she now, Post-3 War? Still alive? Bombed dead? Bewildered because they promised her – promised all the children of the war – that their own children, their children's children would never face war again?

By 1960 it had looked like melt-down. Cuban Missile Crisis, 1961. President Kennedy making a speech, 1963 – problems man-made, therefore man can solve his problems.

1960. The beginning of my world. My mother – love's image and love's loss.

They came past, out into the Playa and on, through into the no man's land that separates Tech from Wreck. On the other side of the railway carriages, they stood facing the Peace Force, in their riot gear, a solid, well-armed humanoid wall of Plexi-shields, full-facers, batons and guns.

One of the mutants, a man with what was left of a tattoo now stretched like barbed wire across his chest where he had bloated with fluid, broke the rank of his kind and stepped forward, right up to the immobile line. He tapped on the head-visor, tried to force it open. The wearer did not move. There was no violence – no sign of life at all.

The big, bloated man opened his mouth and laughed. 'Toxic,' he said, 'me or you?' He laughed, and spat a gobbet of something fermenting on to the sleek face of the helmet. He turned his back to turn away. Someone shot him.

Then it happened.

From the tops of the carriages, hundreds of Wreckers started hurling petrol bombs into the troops. The troops charged the carriages. The tanks came forwards. The helicopters dropped Tear Gas.

I ran down the steps of the tower and into the Playa. Chic X on the low-loader were throwing semi-automatics from crates piled behind the speakers. A woman was carrying grenades in a red plastic laundry basket.

I didn't want a gun, I didn't want a grenade, I wanted to get away.

The old man was sitting where I had left him – he didn't seem afraid.

'The tanks are coming in', I said. 'You can't stay here.'

He got up. He was slow. There was no running to be done.

I saw the small boy with the small dog. 'Go back into the Forest', I shouted, but he stood still, wouldn't move.

There was a blast overhead – deafening – and a rain of slate, metal, wood. I slung Spike on my back, grabbed the boy by the wrist – he had no left hand – and pulled him with me, through the noise, out of the Playa.

There were others fleeing, black shapes with bundles. Our progress was slow, but it didn't matter: the Wreckers were hard to fight, they were organized, no one was coming after us.

Out now, through the dark so dark that the sky and the land slope into each other, stars like hand-holds, marking the way, the way someone has been before.

I should be safe in the city, watching the news in my flat, watching the troubles happening elsewhere, a regrettable and unavoidable clean-up operation; insurgents, terrorists, rule of law and order.

I shouldn't be here, fugitive, lost, but time has become

its own *tsunami*, a tidal wave sweeping me up, crashing me down. You can change everything about yourself – your name, your home, your skin colour, your gender, even your parents, your private history – but you can't change the time you were born in, or what it is you will have to live through.

This is our time.

The small boy was whimpering. I gave him the bottle of milk. He knelt down and poured some into his one good cupped hand, and gave it to the dog to drink. When he had done that with half of the milk, he drank the rest straight off. We went on.

I knew we would come back to the telescope.

Far out, too far to see with the human eye or to hear with the human ear, is everything we have lost. We add to that loss feelings that are unbearable. Send them out into deep space, where we hope they will never touch us. Sometimes, in our dreams, we see the boxed-up miseries and fears, orbiting two miles up, outside our little world, never could rocket them away far enough, never could get rid of them for ever.

Sometimes there's a signal, and we don't want to hear it: we keep the receiving equipment disused, we never updated the analogue computer. Shut off, shut down, what does it matter what happens if we can't hear it?

But there it is – repeating code bouncing off the surface of the moon. Another language, not one we speak – but it is our own.

I don't want to recognize what I can't manage. I want to leave it remote and star-guarded. I want it weightless, because it is too heavy for me to bear.

Sometimes I think it would be better if I had no feelings

at all. Like Spike, I could be neural and not limbic. Like her, I would have no need of emotion. I associate feeling with sadness; and sadness is a void, my empty space. Feeling is empty space. But space is not empty.

Above me, the sky is drilled with stars, ancient light, immense distances, new worlds. If we found another planet, we could leave everything behind, start again, be safe. It would be different, wouldn't it? Another chance.

There's my father leaving for Ireland. There are the Pilgrim Fathers sailing for America.

The new world – El Dorado, Atlantis, the Gold Coast, Newfoundland, Plymouth Rock, Rapanaui, Utopia, Planet Blue. Chanc'd upon, spied through a glass darkly, drunken stories strapped to a barrel of rum, shipwreck, a Bible Compass, a giant fish led us there, a storm whirled us to this isle. In the wilderness of space, we found . . .

The telescope was tilted. The beacon at the tip of the radio antenna was lit up. There was a light on in the hut.

'I am picking up the signal', said Spike.

The old man was standing, hands in his trouser pockets, looking from the dish to the hut. He went towards it, opened the door. He went inside. I could see his shape moving across the window. He seemed to be talking to someone.

'Billie,' said Spike, 'why are you crying?'

'Because it's hopeless, because we're hopeless, the whole stupid fucking human race.'

'Is that why you are crying?'

'And because I wish there was a landing-place that wasn't always being torn up.'

'Is that why you are crying?'

'And because I feel inadequate.'

'There's a story about a princess whose tears turned to diamonds.'

'I'm not a princess and my tears are tears like everyone else's.'

'But they are not everyone else's, Billie. They are your tears.'

And my tears are for the planet because I love it and because we're killing it, and my tears are for these wars and all this loss, and for the children who have no childhood, and for my childhood, which has somehow turned up again, like an orphan on my doorstep asking to be let in. But I don't want to open the door.

'Billie,' said Spike, 'leave me here and go on.'

'I'm not leaving you. Go where?'

'Find your way home.'

'It's not home – it's where I live. That's different.'

'At least you have somewhere to live.'

I looked at the small boy and the small dog. 'I could take them with me.'

'They wouldn't let you look after them. They'd take the boy to hospital, where he will die, and they will have the dog put down.'

'Yes . . .'

'They'll say it's in the best interests of the boy.'

'Yes . . .'

'But it will break his heart.'

'Yes.'

'And his heart is the one thing they haven't broken.'

'Spike?'

'Yes?'

'Why do you say these things now?'

'I am among humans.'

239

'That must be depressing for you.'

'I can't be depressed.'

'No . . .'

'But I will learn.'

'Spike – this is never going to work. Humans can't do it – either we kill each other or we kill the planet or both. We'd destroy the lot rather than make it work.'

'It's taken you a long time to get here.'

'Sixty-five million years since the dinosaurs.'

'That's when the signal was sent.'

'What?'

'It is dated.'

'I thought you couldn't read it.'

'I can.'

'What does it say?'

'It doesn't say anything as such. It is one line of programming code for a Robo *sapiens*.'

The old man came out of the hut. He was waving his arms, excited. We went over to him. The room was humming. 'The analogue computer is driving the dish,' he said. 'I have found what can only be described as a message in a bottle – except that it isn't in a bottle, it's in a wavelength.'

When we approached it, polar-swirled, white-whirled, diamond-blue, routed by rivers, we found a world still forming. There was evidence that carbon had once been the dominant gas, and after that methane and, finally, oxygen, thanks to the intervention of cynobacteria. Oxygen creates a planet receptive to our forms of life.

Like Orbus, Planet Blue is made up of land and sea areas, with high mountain ranges and what appear to be frozen regions. We have landed two roving probes on the planet and expect a steady supply of data over the coming months. The planet is abundantly forested. Insect life, marine life and mammals are evident. It is strikingly similar to our own planet, sixty-five million years ago, with the exception of the dinosaurs, of which we have no record on Orbus.

'A new planet', he said. 'Imagine what we could do if we found a new planet.'

There it is, travelling through the sky, the winning ball with the lucky number on it – not the proto, the almost, the maybe, but this one, Planet Blue, which wanted life so much she got it.

Ranging through the wrecks of stars, burned and blasted, would you find it, alone in the Milky Way, a landing-place?

And if you did find it?

The old man was sitting at the data-print of the computer. I took the manuscript out of my bag, dropped the pages, picked them up again, shuffled as a pack of cards.

'What's that?' Spike asked.

'It's what I told you about, today, yesterday, when, I don't know when, it seems a lifetime ago. *The Stone Gods.*'

'I wonder who left it there?'

'It was me.'

'Why, Billie?'

A message in a bottle. A signal. But then I saw it was still there . . . round and round on the Circle Line. A repeating world.

Is this how it ends?
 It isn't ended yet.

★

'The book isn't finished, but this is as far as I could go.'

'What shall I do with it?'

'Read it. Leave it for someone else to find. The pages are loose – it can be written again.'

In the cave, with Spike, watching the snow fall, watching the snow fall like Leonids, sparking and starting new worlds that last a second, return, re-form, begin again, I wondered if there is a place beyond this, where the dark dice didn't play, where life itself became the winning number, not gambled away later by people like us who valued life so little that we lost it.

A human society that wasn't just disgust.

Noises of whooping and drumming, celebrating the finding of the Egg, as tho' one oaf with a stolen prize could change life and its lot. It will proceed as before: the fighting, the killing, the lack, the loss, for power, for envy, for every stupidity that man can devise.

And here, on my knees, is the little world I wanted to hold for ever, lightly, as the world itself is held in the sky lightly, without threats or fears, without supports of any kind, its own self, a garden of great beauty in a field of stars.

Holland, he said, pointing to a star nearest the moon, and I will clip my heart to him there, as a signal of my love. No flag, no territory, no fortress, no claim, but this love.

She did love me, for the forty weeks that I was her captive or she mine. We were each other's conquered land. We were matched in power and helplessness. We were the barter and the prize, what we played for, what we lost. The dark dice, a two and a one, one became two, then two became two ones. A kingdom lost in a single throw. It's risky, but it's our only chance.

Come back one day. I'll know it's you. I can track you because we are the same stuff.

In the cave, last of the light, beginning of the long dark, I held Spike's head while her eyes closed. I drew up my knees to give her the warmth from my body, pulled my coat around her against the cold.

Already the door is opening and he must go within. The timbered ceiling of the long hall is coffered with stars.

It was the last time we were together; her heart and mine. She did love me, love like a star, light years gone.

'Where are you going, Billie?'

If I could tell you that I could tell you everything – everything about me. There are two questions: where have you come from, and where are you going? But the brain doesn't have separate regions for past and future; only the present is differentiated by the brain.

We split time into three parts. The brain, it seems, splits it twice only: now, and not now.

So in the not-now, I can say that I was set adrift in an open boat, and after a while learned how to make a rudder and oars, though I never mastered a sail and its wind. The wind blows where it will, and I have many times arrived at the unexpected.

But I never found a place to land.

I put the pages on the desk, picked up Spike and kissed her lightly on the mouth. Then I put her on top of the pages.

'See you in sixty-five million years, maybe.'
'Billie?'
'Spike?'
'I'll miss you.'
'That's limbic.'
'I can't help it.'
'That's limbic too.'

I set off, away from the telescope, down through the valley and across the plain of the night. I had no direction or real purpose: I wanted to walk until my mind was still. Far off, I could hear the noise of guns and shouting. I would go back when I could, but not now.

A quantum universe – neither random nor determined. A universe of potentialities, waiting for an intervention to affect the outcome.

Love is an intervention.

Why do we not choose it?

I didn't notice the soldiers coming towards me. Two humans dressed as androids, no faces, no soft skin, combat gear, helmets, guns. One of them shouted something from behind his black visor. I couldn't hear, I shook my head. We stood still, the three of us. They didn't come towards me. I smiled, turned, walked on. There was another shout. I walked on. Then I heard three reports in quick succession, and I fell down. There was blood, a lot of blood, a surprising amount of blood, was what I thought – *so much blood that they had to burn the sheet*. No, that was a long time ago.

The moon is full. There's a star just by. That's what I can see from where I am. Then, for a while, I have to close my eyes.

★

When I open my eyes again, I'm at the bottom of the track. My body is lying at an angle. My clothes are muddy. I know I'm bleeding but the wound was always there.

I look down at my body, small and familiar, and I feel affection, and some regret, because I can't go back there again.

I set off up the track, and it's very dark here under the trees, but the gunfire noise has stopped, and I can hear birds, which is strange because it is so dark.

On my left is the broad, active stream with watercress growing in the fast part, and flag iris on the bank, and a willow bending over the water, and a foam of frog spawn, and a moorhen sailing the current.

I know this track, this stream, I've been here before, many times it seems, though I can't say when. The track rises steeply, and I must quicken my pace. Looking back, it's very dark.

Ahead of me, light is breaking through the canopy of the trees, and it is sunlight and daylight, and I push towards it, higher now, as the bank falls away, and the stream far below gains in strength, ready to fall over the clough.

I feel strong and easy. The climb is nothing. I can feel energy like sap in my body. There is nothing to fear.

At the bend in the track, I see what I know I will see: the compact seventeenth-century house, built on the sheer fall of the drop to the stream. There's a water-barrel by the front door, and a tin cup hung on a chain, and an apple tree at the beginning of the garden, where it meets the track.

The stone slates are mossy and green. The fire is burning inside.

I have to open the gate between the house and the track, and as I look back I can see where I have come and how the light pulls away and then disappears.

I have my hand on the gate, but I hesitate for a minute because when I go through I can't come back.

There's a noise – the door of the house opens. It's you, coming out of the house, coming towards me, smiling, pleased. It's you, and it's me, and I knew it would end like this, and that you would be there, had always been there; it was just a matter of time.

Across the gate, your face. You can't come any further. I have to go through. The latch is light. Yes, open it. It was not difficult.

Everything is imprinted for ever with what it once was.

Acknowledgements

Thanks to Philippa Brewster, Lysander Ashton, Dr Teresa Anderson at Jodrell Bank, Diana Souhami, Simon Prosser and his team at Penguin Books, and my agent, Caroline Michel.

He just wanted a decent book to read ...

Not too much to ask, is it? It was in 1935 when Allen Lane, Managing Director of Bodley Head Publishers, stood on a platform at Exeter railway station looking for something good to read on his journey back to London. His choice was limited to popular magazines and poor-quality paperbacks – the same choice faced every day by the vast majority of readers, few of whom could afford hardbacks. Lane's disappointment and subsequent anger at the range of books generally available led him to found a company – and change the world.

'We believed in the existence in this country of a vast reading public for intelligent books at a low price, and staked everything on it'
Sir Allen Lane, 1902–1970, founder of Penguin Books

The quality paperback had arrived – and not just in bookshops. Lane was adamant that his Penguins should appear in chain stores and tobacconists, and should cost no more than a packet of cigarettes.

Reading habits (and cigarette prices) have changed since 1935, but Penguin still believes in publishing the best books for everybody to enjoy. We still believe that good design costs no more than bad design, and we still believe that quality books published passionately and responsibly make the world a better place.

So wherever you see the little bird – whether it's on a piece of prize-winning literary fiction or a celebrity autobiography, political tour de force or historical masterpiece, a serial-killer thriller, reference book, world classic or a piece of pure escapism – you can bet that it represents the very best that the genre has to offer.

Whatever you like to read – trust Penguin.

read more
www.penguin.co.uk